AF244973

Just One Dance

The Billionaire Barons of Texas • Book Three

CHRIS KENISTON

Indie House Publishing

Indie House Publishing

MORE BOOKS
By Chris Keniston

The Billionaire Barons of Texas
Just One Date
Just One Spark
Just One Dance
Just One Take
Just One Taste
Just One Shot
Just One Chance

Hart Land
Heather
Lily
Violet
Iris
Hyacinth
Rose
Calytrix
Zinnia
Poppy
Picture Perfect

Farraday Country
Adam
Brooks
Connor
Declan
Ethan
Finn
Grace
Hannah
Ian
Jamison

Keeping Eileen
Loving Chloe
Morgan
Neil
Owen

Honeymoon Series
Honeymoon for One
Honeymoon for Three
Honeymoon for Four
Honeymoon for Five

Aloha Romance Series:
Aloha Texas
Almost Paradise
Mai Tai Marriage
Dive Into You
Look of Love
Love by Design
Love Walks In
Shell Game
Flirting with Paradise

Surf's Up Flirts:
(Aloha Series Companions)
Shall We Dance
Love on Tap
Head Over Heels
Perfect Match
Just One Kiss
It Had to Be You
Cat's Meow

CHAPTER ONE

"What you need is a man."

Standing over her latest compound mixture, the dropper in her hand fell to the floor as Eve Baron snapped her head around to face her assistant. "Excuse me?"

"You work too hard." Isabel Santorini had been the best compounder, best assistant that Eve had ever worked with. The standard white lab coat did little to hide the woman's gothic wardrobe, complete with heavy combat boots that thudded their way across the commercial linoleum floors. Nor did the plethora of strategically pierced studs along with raven black dyed hair and striking makeup choices give any hint of the brilliant mind that had worked beside Eve since the day she started Le Perfumerie. "I can sense your tension the minute I cross the threshold. You need a good roll in the hay."

"What I need," Eve spun around and handed Isabel a list of her latest choices, "is for you to compound these and leave my love life alone."

"Would love to. If you had one." Isabel flashed a toothy grin. "Love life, that is."

"My love life is just fine. Thank you."

Isabel set a dish of cheese and fresh finger fruits in front of her. "Sure it is. That's why you've been sleeping on the sofa in your office all week."

Eve could do little more than roll her eyes. The woman was right. Eve loved her work, loved being her own boss. From the moment she'd discovered the art of mixing perfumes and that she was darn good at it, better than creating adhesive compounds for safety stickers, she'd strived to build her reputation and her own business. Now it wasn't uncommon that when she worked on a particularly enchanting scent, time would get away from her and she'd crash on the sofa. On the bright side, working crazy long days for stretches at a time kept her from remembering basic necessities like food, which helped keep her in the same size clothes she'd worn since high school. A caring nagger, Isabel made sure that Eve at least didn't starve to death.

"Thanks. I didn't realize I was hungry." Eve popped a morsel of cheese in her mouth.

"For food or men?"

"Will you stop that." The last thing Eve needed now was a romantic liaison.

"I'm serious. Never mind the roll in the hay. When was the last time you went out on a date?"

"Two weeks ago, at the Shelters for Women annual gala."

One pitch black eyebrow lifted high on Isabel's forehead and her charcoal lips pursed in bitter disagreement. "Jack Preston doesn't count. Even though the man is sexy as hell, he might as well be your brother. Heaven knows no honorable man would be willing to cross the line with his best friend's little sister. Especially when the brother is a Baron and has two more brothers to back him up in a brawl."

There wasn't much of an argument she could give. Jack Preston, her brother Kyle's college buddy, had been her go-to date for charity events and weddings for some time now. It made for great photographs, fed the gossip mill to keep her preferred charities in the news, and repelled unwanted gold-digging male attention. Too bad he wasn't available for tonight's Housing for Heroes event. The entire evening was planned around her joint donation with a major cosmetics company for the naming rights to a recent scent creation. Everyone expected the fundraiser to be a bumper crop night for the non-profit that had done so much for struggling veterans. At least for tonight, her grandparents would be in attendance. Not the same as an escort on her arm, but a safe haven nonetheless. Speaking of which, she glanced down at her wrist watch. Three o'clock. If she high-tailed it out of here she'd be able to beat some of the miserable Houston traffic. One of these days she'd move the operation out of downtown, sell her townhouse in the Heights, and set up in a cheaper, less congested northern suburb. Some day.

She tossed a grape in her mouth and a morsel of mozzarella, then scooped the dish into her hand to finish nibbling on her way out the door. "Thanks for the snack, but I need to get moving if I want to wear something other than my lab coat to tonight's banquet."

Isabel stepped back and nodded. Eve was almost out the door when her assistant shouted after her, "If you find a hot bachelor, take him home with you!"

Pepper limping home was the crown on a miserably hot and unproductive day. If today's mishaps were an indication of how tonight would go, Jared Gold was in serious trouble.

"Uh oh." Older than dirt, with legs as bowed as the St Louis arch, there was no man on this planet that Jared would trust with his horses as much as he trusted Randy. "What happened?"

"Good question. We'd barely ridden the first small section of fence on the east pasture when she started favoring one side. I climbed off and checked her shoes, but didn't see anything. I'm guessing she's got a stone bruise. Before we went out this morning, I cleaned out some pebbles from her shoes, but you know how it goes."

Salt and pepper brows buckled under loose locks of cayenne red hair. "You wear your boots out walking her all the way back?"

"Just about." Jared patted the horse's neck and scratched under her jaw. "Didn't want to take any chances."

"Smart man." Randy smiled and reached for the reins. "I'll take a look at her. You'd better be gettin'. Your mama has called me three times in the last hour, looking for you."

"Blast." Jared snapped his fingers and glanced at his phone. Almost five thirty and two missed calls from his mother. "Tonight's that stupid gala. Promised Mom I'd step in for Dad."

"So she said, but isn't this the fundraiser for building homes for troubled or disabled vets?"

Jared nodded.

"Doesn't sound stupid to me."

"No." Jared blew out a long sigh. He stood corrected. The ranch foreman had been like a second father to him for as long as he could remember. Jason Gold was a great dad but had no interest in the ranch that had been in his family since Texas was its own republic. Everything Jared knew about horses and ranching he'd learned first from his Pawpaw, and then from Randy. Everything he'd learned about being a man and a decent human being had come from both his biological and ranch families. "It's a great cause. One I'd be happy to cut a nice check for. It's the dinner and endless superficial chatter that's going to be a stupid way to spend my night."

"Understood." Randy was a cowboy through and through. He'd never survive a night buttoned up in a tuxedo and sipping champagne. Though the way Jared felt at the moment, he wasn't all that sure he'd survive a night dressed like a penguin, making nice to Houston's social elite either.

Handing his horse over, Jared spun around in the direction of the main house. The day he had graduated from A&M, his dad handed him the keys to the front door, all the books for the ranch, including his name on all the banking accounts, and moved himself and his wife into a lush little four thousand square foot house nestled in the heart of a two-acre treed lot in the burbs. Both his mom and dad had never been happier.

His next thought was how hard would it be to talk his mother into finding a last-minute replacement. Even she would understand any human being would be dead to the world after walking for hours across the ranch on foot with a lame horse. Expecting him to dress up and be social was asking a lot under the circumstances.

"About time." The front door barely latched behind him when his mother appeared in the library doorway. "You're not answering your phone." She sniffed the air. "And you need a shower. A long shower." Despite her announcement of his less than pleasant odiferous contribution to the room, she marched straight up to him and kissed him on his cheek. "We don't want to be late."

All dolled up in a sleek black evening gown, her favorite sapphire and diamond earrings with matching necklace, and her hair high on her head in a simple style that showed off the depth of her sparkling sky-blue eyes, he remembered how excited she'd been when he her one and only son agreed to share a night out with her. He simply didn't have the heart to confess how bone tired he was. "I need a few extra minutes."

Her gaze softened and her hand gently cupped his cheeks. "Hard day?"

"You could say that."

Love and concern shone clearly in her eyes. "What happened?"

He shook his head. "Had to walk Pepper home. She's limping."

"Oh, dear." Her expression crumpled with concern. His mom may not have been cut out to be a country girl, but her kindheartedness extended from animals to humans alike. Tonight's charity du jour was for veterans, next week it could be for stray cats. "Nothing serious, I hope."

"Me too. Randy will let me know, but right now a long hot shower would do me good."

"Take a soak. We can be a little late." She rubbed her hand along his cheek again.

Strangely enough, even though he was a grown man who didn't need or want coddling, his mom's loving touch still had a way of making him feel better. There was no way he could disappoint her by asking to skip tonight. Maybe if he were lucky, he could avoid all the annoying people and just spend the night dancing with his mom.

"I'll call for Mary. Have her make you some hot

chocolate. Good for the soul after a hard day." Mary had been the family housekeeper since before Jared was born. She was as devoted to the Gold family as she was to her own.

"Thanks, Mom." Offering a return smile and gentle squeeze of her hand, he proceeded up the winding staircase to the master suite at the end of the upstairs hall. He might have to nix the hot chocolate and down a gallon of coffee instead, otherwise his mom might find him sleeping in his soup tonight. Maybe a fifteen-minute power nap would help.

Collapsed on his bed, eyes closed, he had no idea if he'd fallen asleep or not when a rap sounded at his bedroom door. "Come in."

The door swung open and carrying a tray, Mary smiled at him sweetly. "Your mother asked me to bring you some hot chocolate. I thought you might prefer coffee. Brought the whole carafe."

"Bless you." He pulled himself upright. There were many things in life he had no doubt about, but he wasn't so sure this house could run without Mary. He knew she was getting up there in years. She'd lost her only son and daughter-in-law in a car accident a few years back and was now raising her only grandson. Some days he thought the responsibility of raising a young boy and taking care of him was more than a woman of her age should take on, and then there were times he was convinced with a heart of gold that Mary would outlive them all. At least for tonight, coffee pot in hand, she was his knight in shining armor. Hopefully, for his mother's sake, consumption of the liquid caffeine would be enough to convert him from an exhausted cowboy into Prince Charming.

CHAPTER TWO

So far, the evening was starting out exactly as challengingly as Eve had expected. Her grandparents always drew a reasonable amount of attention, not just because they were prominent citizens in both social and political circles, but because her grandmother could charm the gold from a leprechaun. She had been a tremendous asset to the Governor for his two decades in politics, but Grams only succeeded in attracting more male attention than Eve and the Baron name garnered on their own. Somehow Eve had managed to dodge both Maude Vandemeer's stuffy and thrice divorced son as well as Octopus Hands Healy without insulting anyone or resorting to hiding in the ladies' room. Though she didn't doubt if the evening continued on the same path, she just might spend more time camping out in the john than at their table.

Hopefully, once the cocktail portion of the evening was over and everyone was seated, she, firmly ensconced between her grandparents, would be able to avoid extra attention.

"It's all delicious, isn't it?" Her grandmother sidled up beside her, perusing the tray of hors d'oeuvres a nearby waiter held out for them, then plucked a bite-sized ball of something. "Have you tried these quinoa bites?"

Eve shook her head. She hadn't tried anything yet, except for nursing a single glass of her favorite white merlot.

"The name is awful, but they are scrumptiously delicious." Small plate in hand, Lila Baron pilfered two more quinoa bites onto her dish and smiled graciously at the waiter.

To appease her grandmother, as the waiter turned to face her, Eve popped one in her mouth. "Oh, they are better than one would expect."

"Would I steer you wrong?" Her grandmother laughed that sweet sound that always made others nearby want to laugh with her. "Oh, Margaret Gold is flagging me down. I'll be right back."

Eve nodded and watched her grandmother glide across the room. Considering her age, the lady still held herself straight and tall and moved with the same grace Eve always remembered. One thing was sure, when Eve reached eighty, she hoped to follow in her grandmother's footsteps.

"There you are." The chairperson for the charity benefit came up to her, rubbing her hands together enthusiastically and grinning like the Cheshire Cat. "There is so much buzz over the naming rights for your latest scent. I can not tell you how thrilled we all are that you would be willing to do this for us. After all, you could get stuck with a dud of a name."

The thought had occurred to her as well the first time she'd done such a thing for charity, but they'd found that most people were reasonable about being redirected with a suitably marketable name. The hardest one was when Ginger Harkenrider wanted to name it Hark the Angels. Finally the woman took a shine to Sweet and Spicy, believing it was a take on her name Ginger.

Slowly inching her way deeper and deeper into the corner, Eve nibbled on more quinoa bites and scanned the attendees. She recognized a good many of the people and was fairly certain she also knew which ones would be digging into their wallets tonight for a good cause and which ones weren't spending a dime above the price of their dinner. From where she stood, she spotted a gentleman smiling at her grandmother. Tall, sandy hair and broad shoulders, the guy knew how to wear a tux. Without a clear view of his face, all she could tell was that many a woman tried to capture his sun-kissed hair color from a bottle, and many more women would most likely be trying to get up close and personal with the man tonight. Unless of course he had a wife to run interference. She didn't envy his wife if he had one. If his face was as appealing as his silhouette, she'd have her hands full beating the women away. Another reason Eve was better off single. Men were a handful. Handsome men were mostly attitude. Rich handsome men were simply trouble. Heaven knew that until recently, her brother Kyle was an excellent example of handsome and rich fodder for the tabloids.

Tired of waiting for the man to turn around, Eve dragged her gaze away from her grandmother and the mystery guy. Most likely by the time Grams was done with him, his checkbook would be open and charity coffers would be overflowing. That made her smile. Her back to the crowd, she watched the staff walk away from the latest addition to the hors d'oeuvres table. A caviar bar. Or was it a caviar fountain? Whatever it was, it was caviar, and she loved caviar. Especially with a little cream cheese on not too dry toast. She could graze her way through the entire set up for the rest of the night—to heck with whatever dinner they were serving.

The only challenge to serving herself was the lack of toast. She scanned all around the tower of caviar, spotted the serving bowls of sour cream, another bowl of finely chopped onions, another with minced hard-boiled eggs, and finally, tray after tray of mini pancakes. That was a first for her. "Who the heck serves caviar on pancakes?" It took a few short seconds to decide she had little to lose giving the mini-cakes a try. Dish in hand, she reached for one, spread a bit of caviar on it, then went for a dollop of sour cream. She would have preferred cream cheese, her grandmother's secret, but this would do. Just one little teeny problem. No sooner had she slapped on the sour cream then the flimsy pancake folded over. She barely caught it with her other hand before dropping the whole shebang on the floor. "This is why normal people use toast."

"For what?" A low and husky male voice rolled over her.

The next few seconds seemed to play out in slow motion. Startled by the spine-tingling voice, one hand flew up to her chest, the pancake dropped again, the caviar bathed in sour cream cascaded down the front of her dress and settled not on the floor, but on the voice's very shiny and expensive dress shoes.

"Oh my." Strong hands with long narrow fingers splayed open wide moved in front of her. "I'm so sorry. I didn't mean to startle you."

Stunned by the display of food on her favorite gown, Eve lifted her gaze, not sure who she was more annoyed with, the chef who thought soggy pancakes were good for caviar and sour cream or... Oh dear Lord. Mister broad shoulders and sun-kissed hair.

Way to go, Lamebrain. For over half an hour, since he'd first spotted the lovely blonde across the room, he'd been trying to make his way over to her. There were two kinds of women here tonight. The ones whose hair was teased or sprayed within an inch of its life and whose face was caked in makeup, or the ones with slits from the bottom up or the top down, leaving little to the imagination. And then there were the ones like the classy blonde in the flowing midnight blue strapless gown. Her hair, twisted above her bare shoulders in a simple bun, glistened under the overhead light. High cheekbones with only a hint of rose, and deep blue eyes to match the gown, under lush long lashes, showed off her natural beauty while looking magazine elegant at the same time. The moment she strolled into the hall she'd caught his eye and kept his attention. It had taken this long to get away from his mother's friends and get close enough to see if her left hand bore a keep-away ring.

To his delight, within a few feet, it was clear her left hand was bare of any tell-tale jewelry. Unfortunately for him, it was also busy with the messiest hors d'oeuvres he'd had the misfortune of dealing with. The same hors d'oeuvres that were now dripping down her dress thanks to him. Not sure of what he could do to save face, he pulled his hanky from his breast pocket and handed it over.

Her hands held out to either side, she stared down at her dress before looking up and meeting his gaze.

"I'll be happy to pay the cleaning bill." It was the only thing that came to mind. Normally, he was known for being a smooth talker. As one of Houston's top ten most eligible bachelors five years running, ladies held him in high regard. Tonight, he seemed to have the vocabulary of a nervous teen.

Fire in her eyes, lips pressed tightly into a thin line, she took in a deep breath and shook her head. "It's not your fault." Looking around, she grabbed a single nearby napkin and wiping up the larger clumps of white stuff, shook her head again. "If you'll excuse me, I need to clean up before I have to deal with people."

"Of course." Again, he stretched out his arm with the cotton handkerchief he kept in his pocket. "This might help."

Once more, her gaze lifted from her dress to his face. He had no idea if she was going to accept or slug him. Finally, she nodded and took hold of the hanky. "Thank you."

Another moment and she was gone.

"Close your mouth. You'll catch flies." His mother came up beside him. "Chasing girls away, are you?"

"Hmm?" He turned to see the teasing smile on her face.

"I saw you talking to a woman and then she ran off. Was it something you said?"

"For what?"

"Excuse me?" Amusement gave way to confusion.

He shook his head. "I asked her *for what* and she spilled her caviar on her dress."

"Oh, no." His mom looked over in the direction his mystery lady had run off to. "I think I'll go see if she needs help."

"Good idea." If the woman wasn't giving up on the high brow event and going home, maybe he'd get another chance to talk to her, or at least learn her name. A phone number would be nice, but he couldn't stand here like a stalker waiting for his mother and the beautiful blonde to return. Turning on his heel, he almost bumped into another woman.

"Jared. So glad you could escort your mother tonight. I understand you both are at the same table with the Governor and me." Mrs. Baron slipped her elbow into his and nudged him into walking. "It will be lovely to catch up. You know, rancher to rancher."

"Yes, ma'am."

Lila Baron's grandson Kyle had been one of Jared's regular cohorts in college. It was actually rather ironic that the two families lived side by side yet Jared hadn't had the opportunity to get to know any of the Baron grandkids until he met Kyle in college. But, as much fun as they often had, eventually Jared had a hard time keeping up with the jet-setting racer and balancing the ranching life he truly loved. Especially once his dad turned the reins over to him.

Seated at the table with one of his mother's longtime charity cronies, he kept an eye out for his mom and the blonde. When they finally appeared in the doorway to the banquet hall, his heart rate kicked into high gear. To his delight, his mother, bless her, was escorting the woman who'd captured his attention to their table.

Pushing to his feet, he waited for the two women to close the distance. Despite plastering on his best winsome smile, the blonde's only response was wide eyed surprise. Surprise that teetered on shock, and he was pretty sure not in a pleasant way. There was another thing he was pretty sure of, it was going to take more than a picture perfect smile and an offer of dry cleaning to get himself out of the dog house.

Lila Baron's eyes widened in a bookend image of the blonde's surprise. "Eve, what happened to the front of your dress?"

His mom waved the older woman's comment off. "A little mishap. It will be dry in no time. Right, dear?"

So the beautiful blonde was Eve, one of the dozens of Baron grandkids, and if his memory served him correctly, Kyle's kid sister. Only now there was nothing little kid about her anymore. Not one bit.

With a smile clearly meant for her grandmother, since she'd made no effort to smile for anyone else, Eve patted the older woman's arm. "Mrs. Gold is correct. By the time we're done with the salad my dress will be dry and no one will know I just took a caviar bath."

Her grandmother's mouth dropped open again before she snapped it shut. "Excuse me?"

"It wasn't that bad." His mother waved another dismissive gesture. "Just a few dribbles."

"I see." Mrs. Baron looked from her granddaughter's dress to her face and then with a small nod, sprouted her own smile. "As Tom Hanks said in *Apollo 13*, looks like we've had our one glitch for tonight."

Jared briefly glanced in the woman's direction. From the frown that Eve suddenly sported, he suspected that she was thinking the same thing he was. That line in the movie came just before one of the worst space disasters of all time had kicked off.

"I see the waiters are beginning to serve dinner. I don't mind admitting I'm famished." Lila Baron tapped the seat next to her and smiled again at her granddaughter. "Come sit between Jared and me. This way you'll have someone young to talk to."

Eve's face was quite expressive as shock once again took over. "You're Jared Gold?"

Not for the first time, his reputation obviously preceded him. Expelling a long sigh, he had no choice but to nod and hope for the best. "Guilty as charged."

CHAPTER THREE

Next time Eve was going to have to remember that if Jack Preston couldn't escort her to a major charity gala, she should just stay the heck home. It wasn't like her latest scent wasn't going to bring in big bucks at auction if she wasn't there to pimp it. Tonight was serious business and being saddled all night with one of her brother's playboy cohorts was not how she wanted to spend an already difficult evening.

"I'm sorry." Her grandmother frowned. "Do you two not know each other?"

Jared cleared his throat. "I'm sorry to say we've only just recently met."

"You could say that." Eve did her best to offer a friendly smile, but she still wasn't completely convinced she'd have spilled the caviar down her dress if he hadn't shown up when he did. She extended her hand. "Eve Baron. Nice to officially meet you."

"The pleasure is all mine."

The waiter appeared with a tray of salads and as Mrs. Gold took her seat, Eve realized that she was designated to sit between her grandmother and Jared. Just what she didn't need tonight, a handsome man with not only a history of partying hard, but a voice as smooth as silk and terribly distracting.

Halfway through the salad, her grandfather engaged Jared in a lengthy conversation about two season breeding. Spring and Fall. She'd been a part of the ranch family her whole life and somehow had missed that the family ranch, like the Gold ranch, had a bumper crop of calves not once but twice a year. The conversation continued with small detours to feed and fence lines for most of dinner. She'd barely had time to close her knife and fork when Jared leaned in and softly said, "Dance with me?"

She glanced over her shoulder at the dance floor. At least other couples had already finished their meals and began moving around the square wooden surface. For a few seconds she considered options for politely declining. Wishing that the MC for the evening would cut off the music and start the auction, she knew as well as anyone else that it was in the charity's best interest to juice up all the attendees with food and alcohol. Two things that helped open checkbooks and increase profits.

"What a lovely idea." Her grandmother turned to her husband and gently lay her hand on his as he regaled the person to his other side about the current political climate in Texas versus back in his day. "Governor, shall we dance?"

The old man turned to his wife and glancing down at her gentle touch on his hand, he smiled up at her and pushed to his feet. "It would be my absolute pleasure."

Before Eve could react, Jared was on his feet, his hand extended in front of her. Despite every alarm in her head screaming for her to say no, that men this good looking and as rich as the Golds could only mean trouble, she was too polite and thoughtful to do anything except nod and follow Jared to the middle of the dance floor. His grip on her hand firm but not too tight, his other hand at the base of spine held her close, but not too close. The man took one step, the pressure on her back increasing as he urged her along and her heart leapt.

If nothing else, the man could dance. Really dance. They'd done a full turn around the dance floor, gliding in perfect synchronization. He even managed to throw in a twirl or two and she didn't trip over her own feet, or his. In college she'd dated a guy who had the unpleasant nickname of twinkle toes. She loved how well he danced and that he'd taught her. He, on the other hand, had hated the nickname and finally opted to change majors and colleges and she was left dating guys who on a good day swayed awkwardly to music.

"Thank you."

"For what?" She tipped her chin upward to better see his face.

His eyes danced with merriment. "That was my line."

It took her a few moments to connect the dots. Those where the unexpected words that had startled her into spilling her caviar the second time. "It was, but thank you for what?"

"Not throwing your dinner in my face when I asked you to dance."

"Well. That wouldn't have been very lady-like, would it?"

"So you did consider it." His smile broadened and the twinkle in his eyes brightened.

She couldn't help but chuckle. "Not quite."

"All the more reason to thank you for this dance."

The choice of words made it sound like he was going to return her to the table when the song ended, and much to her surprise, she was more disappointed at that prospect than she had been upset at the unpleasant accident. "It's nice to take a turn around the floor with someone who doesn't step on my shoes or my dress."

His head tipped back and he chuckled from deep in his chest. "I try my best."

The sound made her tummy do flip flops. All she could think was thank heavens she didn't have to balance caviar while dancing. The deep timbre of his voice would have easily had her spilling on herself all night.

"Your best is pretty darn good. Trust me, I know of which I speak. Four big brothers. All of whom practiced, and I use that word lightly, with me as teens and after all these years, I still may have bruises to prove that all except Mitch have two left feet."

"My mother insisted the mark of a truly happy man is one who can take his wife dancing."

Quickly her brain scurried in an effort to remember if their ranching neighbor was married or not. While Kyle had become famous on the racing circuit, Jared had been one of Houston's society favorite bachelors, whose name was often linked with some woman or other. From what she could remember, nothing about a wedding, to which she was positive at least her grandparents would have been invited, came to mind. "How's your mom's philosophy working out for you?"

He shrugged. "No complaints from the dance floor, but no wife either. Despite Mom's best efforts."

"Ah. You have one of those too?"

"Mothers?" His eyebrows rose high on his forehead.

She bit back a hearty chuckle. "Matchmakers."

"Sadly, yes. And bless her heart, she has the absolute worst perception of who is perfect for me."

"Do we dare compare stories? Because my grandfather has tried some doozies on all of us. One reason why none of us ever show up to an event stag if we can avoid it."

"I gather tonight was unavoidable?"

She nodded.

His grin bloomed again. "Then I guess this is my lucky night."

And with that, he spun her around in an easy twirl and on the song's last note, dipped her back and low. Dang, could this guy dance. Heaven forgive her, but she couldn't help but wonder what other talents did Mr. Sun-kissed Hair have?

For a split second, Jared second guessed himself on that last move. The song and the timing, along with the conversation, was the perfect combination to dip his dance partner. The problem of course being that not all dance partners liked it, especially ones he'd just met and only danced with once. To his immediate relief, the bright flush of her cheeks and huge grin to match told him that he'd done the right thing.

"Oh, my." Hand on her chest, Eve was still grinning. "Not sure I've ever been dipped before."

"You could have fooled me."

"I beg your pardon?" Her smile slipped.

"It's easy for a lady to throw all her weight back on me. You held your weight, making the dip easy."

"I see." A deep crease formed between her brows before she chuckled. "I think."

"I promise it was a compliment."

"Then I'll quit while I'm ahead."

The band started another tune and his gaze darted from her to the band and back. "Up for another turn?"

Her head bobbed quickly.

Once again, they took the standard position of coupled dance partners. "I guess these charity galas are old hat for you?"

Still smiling, she nodded. "Two things happen to a Baron on her sixteenth birthday. The expected coming out party, followed by an introduction to philanthropy 101. Just in case you wanted to know, thanks to two summers straight of volunteering to build homes for veterans, I wield a mean hammer."

"I'll remember that the next time I'm fixing the fence line."

She chuckled. "That I learned long before my sixteenth birthday."

"You're not kidding, are you?" He couldn't picture such a classy woman riding and repairing fence lines.

"All the Baron grandchildren were raised to follow their dreams. Even though we're a family of businessmen, politicians, and adrenaline junkies, each and every one of us know our way around cattle."

It took a second, but he actually began to picture her in denim and cowboy boots, high on a horse, a wide brimmed Stetson shading her deep blue eyes from the sun. "I just bet you do."

"What about you? I don't remember seeing you at the same functions as your mom."

He shook his head. "My charitable upbringing was different from yours. Mom always loved the nitty gritty of helping, but other than donning a tuxedo at her side, Dad's philanthropic efforts consisted mostly of signing checks. I seem to have inherited Dad's charitable genes."

She chuckled. "Good. Then I hope you plan to sign a nice fat check tonight."

Laughter erupted from deep in his gut. "Touché. A nice fat check will be all yours."

For the rest of the dance, Eve filled him in on the details of this evening's charity event. He understood why so many organizations wanted her on their side. Before the last note of the song was played, she'd had him not only convinced that a nice fat check was in order, but had him eager to sign on the dotted line.

"Ladies and gentlemen," a woman's voice replaced the music. "If Miss Baron would kindly step forward. She'll bring us up to date on tonight's special auction item."

His head snapped around in time to see the heave of her chest with a deep breath and her shoulders stiffen. He recognized a person steeling themselves for something they'd rather not be doing. He had the feeling as good as she was at selling her charity, she'd rather be doing it one on one.

"If you'll excuse me, it looks like I'm on." She smiled softly, barely touched his arm and as she strode past him, she paused and glanced over her shoulder at him. "Thanks. That's the most fun I've had in a long while."

He should have said something, but his tongue seemed to have gone numb. Instead, he nodded and hoped there'd be time for another dance and a chance to get her number.

"She is lovely." His mother's voice carried over his shoulder.

There was no point in arguing. As he'd done with Eve a moment ago, he nodded.

"We might as well take our seats." His mother set her hand on his shoulder. "Coming?"

"Of course." It took more effort than it should have to drag his gaze away from the swirl of Eve's gown as she walked away from him.

Settled in next to the Baron matriarch, he didn't have to worry about polite chit chat, everyone's eyes were riveted to the stage. Her smile bright, her shoulders straight, her gown flowing, Eve could easily have been a superstar of the golden era of films about to accept an award.

"Good evening, ladies and gentlemen." At the podium, her gaze shifted to specific tables. "I'm delighted to be here with y'all tonight."

An eruption of applause momentarily filled the room.

"As you have had plenty of time to peruse the auction tables, you know we have some wonderful items available this evening."

To Jared's surprise, there was little murmuring or other sounds that came with a banquet room filled with rich and by now, slightly tipsy potential donors. Or in this case, bidders. As she went through the list of the larger ticket items and thanked the donors, he could see who was here for the cause, and who was here to be seen, or even patted on the back. When she got to the part of naming the latest scents that would be marketed by one of the largest cosmetic companies in the country, the room grew suddenly more silent.

"I'm especially proud of this evening's perfume. I love having grown up in Texas. We are so blessed with natural wonders and fabulous flowers."

He had to give her credit, she was selling the room on something everyone could relate to. There was a reason the expression *everything's bigger in Texas* had taken root in the state's culture.

"It was last year during a visit to Tyler's rose festival that I remembered my Grams and how everything she touched always smelled of rose water. Our Texas roses brought that sweet scent to life for me and it has taken me over a year to capture just the right combination that will bring a lifetime of happy memories like my Grams gave us."

By the time she'd finished with her subtle but compelling sales pitch, Jared had no doubt that this evening's charity was going to have more money than it knew what to do with.

CHAPTER FOUR

"I understand you were the hit of the evening last night." Whenever Craig's business brought him to the Houston area, he did his best to spend some time at the ranch. Lucky for Eve, this was his weekend. Her brother poured a cup of coffee and took a seat beside her.

"If you mean I didn't get a minute to myself after my on-stage pitch, then yes." All she'd wanted the rest of the evening was another chance for a dance with Jared Gold. Unfortunately, every potential donor under the sun had come forward to visit, chat, and eat away any hope she had of a last dance before Margaret Gold and her son had quietly slipped away.

"Don't you listen to her." A tail wagging puppy, curled up comfortably on her lap, love and pride shone in Lila Baron's eyes as she smiled at her granddaughter. "She was indeed a hit and the naming rights for the new scent broke the bank. Even with increasing costs, there will most definitely be more homes for our struggling veterans."

"I also heard you were seen being dipped by Jared Gold." This time, eyeing her over the brim of his coffee cup, her brother failed to hide his impish grin. He knew full well men like Jack Preston and Jared Gold weren't her type.

"We danced." She hoped the heat in her cheeks wasn't giving away the girlish interest in a man who dipped her off her feet. She should probably remind herself as well that nothing good ever came from playing with fire. "Just one dance." Much to her chagrin. "Nothing to get all gossipy about." Any minute now she expected someone to call her out and shout *Liar, liar, pants on fire.*

"Then," Craig put his cup down on the saucer, "you

won't care that Jared called this morning."

"Oh." Did her voice crack?

"Yeah." Craig bit back a smile. "He might have mentioned something about stopping by."

"Here?" Great, she went from a cracked voice to a squeaky voice.

"I'm pretty sure he didn't mean my place in Austin."

"Oh." Finally, a word in her normal voice. "Then he's coming to see you."

Craig took such a long and slow sip of his coffee it probably would have qualified for a Guinness World record. Eve took a bite of her eggs and did her utmost best to pretend she didn't care one iota what Mr. Sun-kissed Hair did or didn't do.

The doorbell rang and she nearly spit out her food. At this hour on a Saturday, she hadn't bothered with makeup, her hair was clipped in a makeshift bun on the top of her head, and of course she had to throw on a pair of baggy old sweats this morning. Had she known they were having company she would have at least donned something more put together.

"Morning." Craig pointed to the coffee pot on the buffet as their guest entered the room. "Would you like a cup?"

Hat in his hand, Jared nodded. "That would be great. I barely had time this morning to knock back a few sips."

The puppy had leapt off Gram's lap and she and her sibling were now dancing circles around Jared's booted feet.

"Honey. Moon." Grams snapped her fingers at the pups whose wagging rear ends immediately plopped on the floor as they stared up at their mistress. "Please make yourself at home." Grams gestured to one of the empty seats at the table. "This is such a pleasant surprise."

"Thank you." He tipped his head at Eve and smiled. "You were quite the hit last night."

"Told ya." Craig sprouted a toothy satisfied grin. Why he seemed to find this situation so amusing, she didn't quite understand. Normally he'd be chasing off a suitor with a loaded shotgun.

Pouring a tall cup of java, Jared's gaze subtly shifted from Craig to her. Thankfully he had the good manners to leave her brother's comment alone. Instead, his attention turned to her grandmother. "Is the Governor around?"

"I'm afraid not." Grams shook her head. "He had an early meeting this morning. Is it urgent?"

"No." His eyes casually glanced in her direction before returning to the family matriarch. "But one of your bulls has breached the south fence."

"Again?" Grams sighed. "I swear we got an ornery crop of bovine this season."

"I shored it up for now, but it might be time to steel up that section if y'all are going to keep the bulls in that pasture."

"The Governor mentioned something about that at dinner the other night," Craig said.

"Figured since we share the fence line, I needed to talk to your grandfather before I make too many plans."

"You thinking of doing this yourself or hiring out?" Craig asked.

His gaze briefly drifting in her direction, Jared lifted the corners of his mouth in a slight hint of a smile before returning to the conversation with her brother. "I guess that depends on how many of you remember how to work a ranch." Now that essence of a lazy grin sprouted into a full-blown smile.

She resisted the urge to shake her head. Just how she wanted to start her morning, overseeing a pissing contest between two overgrown boys.

The way the muscles in Craig's jawline twitched, she knew the wide smile was a precursor to a testosterone challenge. "Don't need to remember something you don't forget."

Jared bobbed his head. "Good, then we can count on you for a little hard day's work."

"And my brothers."

Oh, weren't her other brothers going to be thrilled to learn that Craig had volunteered them to build a steel fence. She knew for a fact that both the Golds as well as the

Barons could afford to contract a project of that magnitude, but she also knew generations of cowboy genetics, combined with good old-fashioned male DNA, meant these boys were going to have to prove to each other that they still had the right stuff.

The conversation continued long enough for Eve to finish her breakfast and consider whether or not last night's dance had anything to do with this visit. She was pretty sure that normally this sort of business discussion would have happened over the telephone. After all, she had spent a bazillion weekends here in the last decade, and Jared Gold had not once set foot on their doorstep. On the other hand, maybe a large expensive project like this did indeed require face-to-face discussion.

"I hate to eat and run." Craig pushed away from the table. "But I have a meeting with a Hollywood diva who bought the rights to a book and wants us to produce it."

"You don't look very enthused about it," Eve said.

"I'm not. The book is good. Very good. But this is one movie star whose reputation for causing trouble during production has most producers spooked."

Both puppies resting obediently in their beds in the corner of the room, their grandmother slid back from the table and stood. "I have confidence that if anyone can keep this woman in line, it's you." She took a couple of steps, and tenderly brushed her fingertips along his jaw. "You inherited your grandfather's charming ways."

It took everything in Eve not to spit with laughter. While the grandfather she knew could be quite doting on his beloved wife, gruff, determined, and powerful were the sort of words that came to the forefront of her mind when describing the man. Many others came to mind as well, but charming was rarely one of them.

With her brother and grandmother on their feet, Jared, and she followed suit. When she turned to follow her grandmother out of the room, Jared reached for her hand to slow her steps. He fell in beside her, his voice dropping to a near whisper. "Can we talk for a minute?"

"Of course." She stopped in her tracks. "Is something wrong?"

His hat in one hand, he ran the other one roughly across the back of his neck. "I'm sorry. I didn't mean to give that impression." His hand fell to his side, and his weight shifted from one foot to the other. Letting out a deep sigh, and with an almost unnoticeable shake of his head, his eyes settled on hers. "For a grown man, I'm really botching this. I was hoping to get your phone number."

This was a very different side of the cocky man who had just had a verbal sparring match with her brother, and nothing like the reputation of a notoriously charming bachelor. She tried not to smile too widely. "Of course. Let me get my phone and I'll text you."

"Actually." He smacked his hat against his thigh. "Perhaps since I'm already here, I could persuade you to join me for dinner tonight?"

"Oh." For some reason the invitation took her by surprise.

"Or not."

"No, no. Dinner would be...nice." The need to smile tugged at her cheeks until her plans for the day smacked her upside the head. "Except I promised to do a few photo ops with the bid winner and then stay to help out at the current building site this afternoon. I'm not really sure if I'd be able to sneak away early enough."

"Building site?"

"Yes. Last night's charity. A lot like Habitat for Humanity, volunteers work the home construction site. I promised the coordinator last night that I would come. Any publicity is always helpful."

"Could you use some extra hands?"

His response was unexpected, especially after last night's comment about preferring to just cut a check, but she had never been one to look a gift horse in the mouth. "Always, but I'll be leaving here by ten."

He dipped his chin in understanding and she was all set for him to back out and reschedule dinner when he smiled at her. "I'll pick you up." Still smiling, he plopped his hat on his head, and crossing the foyer in three long strides, opened the front door. "See you at ten."

She nodded and watched the door close behind him. The only coherent thought that came to mind was, ten o'clock in the morning couldn't come soon enough.

His foreman was going to love him for bailing on a hard work day, but if the boss couldn't take a day off for a good cause, what good was being the boss. Standing on the Baron front porch, Jared glanced around him waiting for someone to come to the door. He'd always been impressed by the home's resemblance to Tara from the iconic 1939 film. The architecture extravagant for the area and yet, it somehow fit in well with the rolling hills and even the smattering of cows mulling about didn't look out of place.

The door swung open and from over the butler's shoulder, he could see Eve galloping down the front stairwell.

"I'm ready if you are." Her smile was wide, sincere, and utterly captivating. In form-fitting denim and a sharply pressed button-down shirt, she would no doubt be the best dressed construction worker on the continent. That she landed on the ground floor with a thud and trotted over, cheeks flushed and slightly out of breath, only added to her charm.

If he wasn't careful, he was going to be in big trouble. Sooner than later. "I'm all yours."

Her eyes widened slightly and he pinched his eyes shut.

Had he really said something so inappropriately provocative? "I mean, for the day. The work day."

Slipping past him, she chuckled softly. "I got it." The second her eyes landed on his car, she came to a screeching halt. "You drive a Porsche?"

"Is that a problem?"

"No. Not at all. I just expected you to show up in a work truck not a GT-3 RS."

Had she been standing by the insignia he wouldn't have been caught by surprise, but it was pretty clear she recognized the car instantly. This lady was full of surprises. "You know your cars."

"I'd better or Kyle would have my head on a platter."

Of course. It made sense that the sister of a professional racecar driver would know her cars. "Would you like to drive?"

Her head snapped around so fast, any mere mortal could have gotten whiplash. Her eyes rounded with surprise, her mouth hanging slightly open, he wondered if he'd said the wrong thing. "You'd let me drive your Porsche?"

He shifted his gaze from her to his car and back. "Can you drive a stick?"

Her head bobbed.

"Then yes."

Once again her eyes rounded and a slow smile stretched across her face. Extending her arm, she shook her head ever so slightly. "You are an enigma, Mr. Gold."

"Why is that?" He dropped the keys into the palm of her hand.

"For a woman, a car is nothing more than transportation. But for a man, a sports car like this ranges anywhere from his pride and joy to his baby girl. Few men would let anybody drive their treasure. Let's just say, you surprise me."

"Baby girl?"

Curling her fingers around the keys, she practically bounced around the car to the driver door. "Everyone knows cars are named after women. Expensive cars after very beautiful women."

There was no resisting the smile that tugged at the corners of his mouth. He might just have to rename the car Eve.

In only a matter of moments, Eve was buckled in and before he could explain the quirks of the car, she'd shifted gears and took off at speeds even he wouldn't have considered. Any moment he expected them to be airborne and was very thankful the drive was a straight shot or else they just might have found themselves taking the curves on two wheels. "Are we running late?"

Eve shook her head.

"Then there's no hurry?"

"None." At least she kept two hands on the wheel and her eyes on the road.

"So, we don't need to rush?" If it didn't make him feel like his mother, he'd be digging his nails into the dashboard for dear life.

Her gaze left the road and she drilled him with an incredulous glare. "It's a Porsche."

That much he knew.

"These babies were meant to be pushed." Her attention returned to the road ahead. With a touch as gentle as a mama caressing her newborn babe, Eve ran her fingers over the dash and sweetly muttered, "Don't you let the scaredy-cat man hurt your feelings."

"Scaredy-cat?" The urge to steal the keys and show her exactly what his car could do was surprisingly strong.

"Every now and again, a little speed on the open road is good for the soul."

He couldn't argue with her, but it abruptly occurred to him that the need for speed might be a genetic thing. After all, the Baron name was well known in both the auto racing circuit and the sailing circuit. Apparently, the lack of a sense of mortality, and the ability to travel in the fast lane was not limited to the male line of the Baron clan.

CHAPTER FIVE

Every car that Eve had ever owned had been practical. She'd learned to drive on her grandfather's lap at the age of eight. Or was it nine? Well, most people might not consider that learning to actually drive. There were so many roads on the ranch that her grandfather would sit her on his lap and let her steer while he worked the pedals. By the time she was actually old enough to get her permit, handling the old Jeep was easy. On her 16th birthday her dad gifted her a Mustang. The car looked great. Inside she was snug as a bug in a rug. But she never tested what the horsepower under the hood could do. By the time she graduated college, she'd upgraded to a Lexus SUV. Not exactly designed for speed. Since then, she'd been through two more cars, but always a practical vehicle with plenty of cargo space.

Although her brother Kyle had let her drive his Aston Martin the time he'd broken his wrist, she'd known better than to push the limits on the car. It wasn't usual for her to crave speed like her brother, but today, the roar of the Porsche engine and the almost cockpit like design of the interior of the car proved to be irresistible to her dormant lead foot. "This baby really hugs the road."

"Thank heavens for that." Jared winked at her. Now that he was no longer digging his nails into the dashboard, he actually seemed to be comfortable with her driving skills.

At least she thought that's what the wink was for. "I can see why my brother loves his high-performance cars."

"A fine-tuned car is like a master's musical instrument. They need to be played to the fullest and babied at the same time."

She reached the end of Baron land, took the turn on the other side of the archway a little faster than she probably should have, but she simply loved how well the car handled. On the main road leading back to town, she eased up on the gas pedal and noticed the tension in Jared's shoulders ease. "I'm sorry, I probably shouldn't have done that."

"Done what? Drive like Mario Andretti or shave five years off my life expectancy?" The words were harsh, but the tone was playful and the smile on his face told her that he wasn't upset with her. As a matter of fact, if she was reading the sparkle in his eyes correctly, she had a feeling he actually enjoyed being taken for one heck of a short ride.

Lips pressed tightly together, she bit back a laugh. "Both maybe."

The construction site for the new development was just over the highway on the southern border of town. Even driving a hair over the speed limit, it took only minutes to reach the entry and follow the signs to the Housing for Heroes houses. There were three veteran's homes under construction at the moment. One barely past the stage of pouring the foundation. The other fully framed and ready for sheetrock. The third was in the finishing stages of final trim work. She wasn't positive but she felt sure the photo ops would be at the third house and the day's work would be at house number two.

Jared hadn't said a word since they drove through what would soon be the gates to the community, but as she pulled up to the house with the large banner for her pet charity, she detected a hint of a nod. "Thanks for letting me tag along."

Turning the car into the driveway of the almost finished house, she threw the car into first gear, turned off the engine, unbuckled her seatbelt, and turned to face him. "Ready to get down and dirty?"

The way his eyes flashed brightly for a split second, she realized how easily her choice of words could have been interpreted differently than what she'd intended. Only his instant recovery of a placid expression and casual nod as he hopped out of the car and circled the hood to open her door told her that he had no intention of calling her out on the flub. "I'll follow your lead. Let me know when I'm needed."

She appreciated that. "Sounds good."

Thirty minutes later she'd been photographed wearing a hard hat, tool belt, hammering in a nail, carrying a two by four, as well as sawing at a section of base board. When the publicity part of her day was over, she'd expected to find Jared sitting on an upended paint bucket waiting. Instead, she had to go hunting for the guy. Spotting him on a ladder hanging a ceiling fan, she wondered what happened to the man who preferred to write checks.

Finished, he looked over his shoulder and almost caught her staring at him. "There you are. All done with the promo bit?"

"I am." She nodded "Looks like you got to work without me."

"Saw a need and stepped in. All three bedrooms have the fans hung, of course this room here, and now I'm going to screw some bulbs in the kitchen canned lights."

"Sounds easy enough." She paused to look around for the volunteer coordinator. "Did Annabelle or George give you a list?"

He shrugged as his booted foot hit the floor. "Depends on whether or not the foreman in the other room is George."

As if on cue, a man she did not recognize came out and stopped short, his gaze shifting from Jared to her. "May I help you?"

Eve stepped forward and extended her hand. "Eve Baron. I'm here with the volunteer crew."

"Of course." The tall man smiled, shook her hand and nodded. "Nate Tailor. They're working on the house next door."

That caught her by surprise, and judging by the way Jared's brows arched high over wide eyes, she'd guess he didn't expect that response either. If the volunteers were next door, why was Jared hanging ceiling fans in this house?

Another fellow in jeans and a jangling tool belt stomped through the doorway and dropped a very loud and most likely heavy tool bag on the floor at his feet. "I should have stayed in bed. Got caught in a bottleneck on I-45. Tractor trailer overturned."

Nate frowned at him, then looked at Jared. "Who are you?"

"I'm with her." Jared waved a thumb in Eve's direction.

His mouth momentarily twisted to one side, Nate blew out a deep sigh. "You're not the new electrician?"

The guy who had stomped into the house turned to face Jared. "Man, I really should have stayed in bed."

Jared lifted two hands in front of him, palms out, and shook his head. "Just another volunteer. A volunteer who is going to go next door now." He curled his fingers around Eve's arm and quickly led her out the door.

The breeding her family had drummed into her through the decades wouldn't allow her to leave without saying something. Looking over her shoulder as she shuffled after Jared, she smiled at the contractor. "It was nice meeting you, Nate."

The man bobbed his head in acknowledgment and spun quickly to face the electrician.

Out the front door, biting back a grin, she glanced at Jared. "I can't believe you were in the wrong house and he put you to work."

Chuckling under his breath, Jared cleared his throat. "I admit, I was a bit surprised when he handed me the fans without even asking if I knew how to install one."

"But you did it?"

Still grinning, Jared nodded. "Three of them. Anyone can hang a ceiling fan. So I did."

Halfway down the walkway, they heard Nate loudly spouting instructions to check the fan installations along with a few other choice words she had no intention of repeating. As if choreographed, they turned to look over their shoulders at the electrician staring up dumfounded at the living room fan. The two of them nearly doubled over with laughter, and practically ran the rest of the way to the right house.

Out of breath and still giggling at the front door of the

correct house, they were greeted by a surly older man. "What may I ask is so funny?"

"Nothing really." Jared swallowed a smile.

"Nothing at all." Eve confirmed, practically biting her cheeks to keep from laughing.

Jared had no idea why he found the whole house mishap so funny, but he did, and apparently so did Eve. One more reason to like her.

"There you are," a much too happy woman called from behind Mr. Grumpy and hurried up to them. "We've had a low turnout today and could use the extra hands."

A symphony of hammers banging, saws sawing, and drills whirring, sounded to him like plenty of people had shown up.

Eve took a step forward. "Where would you like us to start?"

The lady didn't blink an eye. She pointed in the house and turned on her heel. "There are paint cans in the master bedroom. Whoever is good on ladders can do the trim out and whoever is good with the roller can do the walls. If you need anything, whistle. I'll check in with you shortly." She stopped at the mouth of the hallway, pointed down the hall, then once again, spun around on one foot and marched off.

"I guess we're painting." Jared followed Eve down the hall. "You want to trim or use the roller?"

"I'll do the trim." She stopped short at the bedroom door. "Right after I tape off the room."

This wasn't an elaborate home. It was pretty much off the rack and even Jared knew that for years, builders had taken to painting walls and ceilings in one color to save time and money. The lighter flat ceiling paint was going to make a nice first impression for whoever moved in. It was also going to take more time. "I'll tape the ceiling, you do the baseboard."

She shook her head. "You start opening the paint cans

and covering the floors with those plastic tarps over there. I'll start taping. It won't take long." Without waiting for a response, she glanced around the room. "As soon as I find the tape and a ladder."

In a matter of a few seconds, he'd learned just a bit more about the Baron granddaughter. He wondered if that independent streak was genetic in Barons or the product of having to compete with four brothers. If he were wagering, he'd bet she'd learned to order those four brothers around the way she'd just taken charge of their assignment. Though he shouldn't forget her grandfather was a Marine Corps general. Taking command and handing out orders might have been something she learned on the Governor's proverbial knee.

Eve lifted a bag in the corner by the paint cans. "Found the tape."

"Good. I spotted a couple of ladders in one of the rooms down the hall. Give me a second and I'll see if we can use one."

The serious look on her face eased and a smile bloomed. "Great. I'll start taping the baseboards."

One six-foot ladder in hand, he returned to the room to find Eve had taped off half the room and was making fast progress on the other half. So the woman was independent, a little bossy, and quite competent. Not that the latter should have been a surprise. No one commands the respect she received at the banquet the other night without having accomplished quite a bit. And as far as he knew, incompetent people might be able to fool a few people, but not everyone. Yep. Eve Baron was the real deal in so many ways.

"Done." She straightened to her full height, dangling the roll of painters tape on her wrist.

"Where do you want the ladder?"

"Right here is fine." He set it up and without letting go, looked over his shoulder at her. "Sure you don't want to let me do the ladder work?"

"Positive." She flashed a toothy grin and then waved her thumb to her left for him to move.

He was pretty sure the streak of Texas chivalry prompting him to insist he do the ladder work would not be well received. As a matter of fact, he wouldn't be surprised if insisting didn't find him in a headlock or some other compromising position. Nope. That little recording of his mother's voice playing in his head, nudging him forward to 'help the little lady' was simply going to have to be ignored.

As expected, it didn't take long to develop a comfortable rhythm. He rolled one wall and she trimmed the opposite wall. He'd known she'd said that her family had insisted that all the kids learn to serve others through different charities, and that she had specifically mentioned working on project houses for veterans, but now he could see that she wasn't just there for show. Any professional painter would be pleased to have her on his crew.

Two of the four walls done, and dipping the roller in the five-gallon bucket, he caught a flash of movement in his peripheral vision. One hand on the still unpainted wall, Eve was leaning way too far to the side.

"Whoa." He poised to catch her if the ladder tipped. "If you fall off that ladder, they're not going to let you come back." He leaned the roller handle against the wall. "Let me move that for you." Steel gray eyes pierced him like a sharp dagger. *Or maybe not.* "Please, just be careful."

That bright smile was back and he couldn't help but return the smile. Their timing was perfect. Halfway done with the last wall and she'd finished the upper trim.

"All done." She set the brush in the jug of paint she'd been using and one hand on the ladder, climbed down. Except halfway, her foot slipped off the step and he could see her and the ladder wobbling.

Paint be damned, he dropped the roller and took a leap forward just in time to catch her in his arms as the ladder slammed over onto the floor. "You okay?"

Snuggled against his chest, Eve dared to look up at him. "I think I missed a step."

"Ya think?" he teased.

"And I may have spilled a little paint."

He glanced down at the splatters on the concrete floor.

It could have been worse. She could have been carrying a full jug. "A little."

"I guess it's a good thing the floors go in last."

"I guess," he chuckled, unable to tear his gaze away from the sweet eyes staring up at him.

"Everything okay in here?" The coordinator popped her head into the room.

Still holding Eve in his arms, Jared spun around to face the woman.

"Just fine," the two muttered in chorus, breaking into a new fit of giggles. Clearly, they both found remodeling homes pure entertainment. Or maybe it was the company.

The lady nodded her head, smiled, and walked away. Apparently laughing volunteers carrying other volunteers was nothing new or surprising to her. But the most interesting part of the whole thing…he really was fine. More fine than he'd been in a very long time.

CHAPTER SIX

"Yes." Eve knew she shouldn't agree to adding anything new to her calendar. The last couple of months, work had been keeping her at the lab later and later, and her charity work took up what little time she had left. No way she had time to do one more lick of volunteer, charity, or any other work. Yet, here she was saying yes. Again. "My pleasure, Mrs. Kessler."

Eve slid her phone into her pocket and wondered if maybe it didn't make more sense to just throw the dang thing under a sofa cushion with the ringer turned off.

From the head of the massive family dining table, her grandfather looked up. "Bad news?"

She shook her head. "No. I'm just going to be helping stuff and sort backpacks for the beginning of school."

The Governor smiled. "If you need more help, I'm sure your grandmother would love a task like that."

"Too late. Grams is already on the volunteer list." At least her grandfather was right. Anything that benefited children, whether it was signing a check or getting her hands dirty, her grandmother was always on board. That particular tendency was just one of many about her grandmother that always brought a smile to Eve's face.

"You do seem to be burning the candle at both ends." Her cousin Devlin glanced up from the table and waggled one brow at her. "Late nights. Early mornings."

"And how would you know that?" Eve loved that her family cared for each other, but it irked her to think her business was everyone else's business.

Dev waved a fork in Chase's direction.

"Hey," Chase blurted, staring down his cousin, "I can

get into trouble with my sister all by myself. I don't need you throwing me under the bus."

Tossing his hands up in the air, Dev shook his head and smiled. "You said it, not me."

"All right, children." Eve had too much on her mind now, including one very tall, handsome, and interesting rancher, to deal with squabbling relatives. "Y'all can duke it out after lunch."

"Yeah," Eve's half sister Paige waved at her brother and cousin. "I want to hear more about you and the gorgeous neighbor."

Paige was a few years younger than Eve, and having inherited the Baron business sense, she had turned the family vineyard from a floundering concept into an award-winning winery, but some days the inner teen reared its curious head. Under normal circumstances, when Paige was interrogating one of their brothers, Eve didn't mind so much, but she didn't like her love life, or in this case lack of one, to be the center of attention. She was all set to tell Paige there was nothing to say, when it struck her that the word gorgeous was thrown around. "You've met Jared?"

"I don't know that met is the right word, but I've spotted him a time or two chatting with the Governor. Let me tell you, that man knows how to wear a pair of jeans."

That he did, but Eve wasn't going to go there with her kid sister. "I wouldn't know."

She and Paige were the only two women at the table and right about now the conversation had the men's full attention. Not even the puppies waddling from person to person hoping to catch food droppings could snare the men's attention. Not that they cared how Jared looked in worn blue jeans, but she knew they were reading her every reaction. Ever since she was old enough to shed her braces, her brothers and cousins watched over her like a hawk. Especially when a member of the opposite sex with a history of carousing with Kyle was flittering around her.

Craig in particular had that left eyebrow cranked higher than the right. He wasn't buying a word she said and she knew it. The other day he was simply having fun teasing her, but now he seemed to have a different take on the situation. Maybe it came from years of producing shows and movies, but the guy had a malarkey radar like no one else in the family. "So, when are you seeing Jared next?"

"I'm not."

That eyebrow shot impossibly higher. "You don't say?"

Paige's eye's sparked with interest. "So there *is* something going on?" Her shoulders hitched in a moment of enthusiastic delight. "This calls for a girls' night. I want to hear it all. Things have been too quiet on the romantic front."

"There is no romantic front." Eve did her best to slip on a relaxed smile, even though she felt like a witness on the stand about to be pelted by opposing council. "He simply volunteered his time for a worthy cause the same way the rest of us do. Often."

"Wait." Mitch hadn't been at breakfast yesterday. "You mean there's more going on than the two of you playing Fred and Ginger the other night?"

Some days she had a really big mouth.

"See?" Paige said with a bit too much glee in her voice. "Finally, someone's broken the dry spell."

"Dry spell?" Mitch looked to one of his two youngest sisters, then scanned the table. "What am I missing?"

"That your sister works too darn hard and doesn't have time for dating. None of us do." Paige's playful tone slipped into one more suited for the general manager of a profitable Texas winery. The teasing teen little sister was gone, and the grown-up lioness defending her pack was on alert. "If she's finally found a hunk to hook up with, good for her."

All the men's eyes rounded and Mitch's jaw dropped, no words forming.

"Okay." Eve raised her hands. "No one is hooking up with anyone. It's just a case of good neighbors doing the charitable thing. It's over. Move on." She picked up her fork and dipped it into the blueberry pie, intentionally not looking at her siblings. This was one time she did not want to read the room.

"I don't know about that." Craig lifted his gaze to the

massive plate glass window that overlooked the front drive. "I believe this may be the first time in history our dear neighbor has crossed our doorstep two days in a row."

"What?" Her eyes shot up and sure enough, Jared hopped out of a jeep and trotted up the front steps. *Oh, boy.*

Ever since they'd left the Hero's project, he'd been haunted by the idea of how badly some of the veterans' kids were hurting. All during his morning chores his mind kept tripping over imaginary faces of lonesome children. When he rode out to his favorite pasture, for the first time in years he was reminded how painful it had been as a small boy to lose his grandparents. Those two had lived and breathed the Gold ranch and shared that love with Jared. He couldn't have been more than three when his grandfather sat him on his first horse. Small for a horse, to Jared, Saffron had seemed as big as a Clydesdale. Probably bigger.

When his parents sat him down in the parlor that miserable morning to explain that his Grammy and Grampy had been killed in an accident on the freeway, he hadn't truly understood what being dead meant. Once the permanence of their absence finally struck him, he'd had no idea how badly a heart could hurt. This morning, staring out at the green landscape as far as the eye could see, memories of Randy taking him along as he worked, in a way, picking up the reins from his Pawpaw, filled him with the same peace and comfort working at Randy's side had done all those years ago. Jared couldn't imagine overcoming the sadness that had so deeply overwhelmed him without the ranch, the horses, and Randy.

Now, all he could think was that for some of these kids whose dads were struggling with PTSD and other post war issues, the hurt had to be as deep and confusing as it had been for Jared. All morning he'd kicked this crazy idea around in his head. The debate between a fabulous idea and sheer insanity had continued from the first spark right up to when he'd grabbed his car keys out of the bowl on the entry table. Despite having told himself he was not going to bother Eve, here he was. All the arguing with himself in the world hadn't stopped him from turning down the main road and circling around to the Baron archway onto one of the biggest ranches in South Texas.

Once he'd turned down the drive his common sense kicked in and insisted that calling was the more appropriate thing to do. Except halfway down the Baron driveway, common sense didn't have a chance of winning over the driving urge to see her face to face again. Share his idea. Ask for her thoughts. Maybe even her help. He didn't quite know what to make of it. This would not be the first time he'd been infatuated with an attractive woman, but it most certainly was the first time that a hard morning's work couldn't drive the woman out of his thoughts. He was most definitely, as his mother would say, smitten.

His hand poised to knock, the massive front door slowly swung open. Expecting to see one of the help, he was surprised to find the Governor himself at the door. "Hello, sir."

To his relief, the Governor sprouted a sincere smile. "Hello. Have you eaten?" The older man stepped aside and waved him in.

"Yes, sir." Hat in hand, Jared twirled it round. "I was hoping to catch Eve in."

"Of course. The Baron dining room is the most likely place to find my troops on a Sunday."

The old guy wasn't exaggerating. The Baron homestead was most likely one of the few houses in Texas that still used a formal dining room with a table long enough to be viable at Buckingham palace.

"Eve, you have a caller."

"Hello." Down on one knee, he scratched at the puppies once again dancing at his feet. He stopped and straightened to his full height when face to face with Eve, "I was hoping you might have an hour to spare. I've been mulling over a business idea and would like to run it by you."

Eve's eyes opened wide. "Me?"

He bobbed his head. "It's about the Housing for Heroes."

"Oh." She jumped up from her seat. "No problem, we can use the Governor's office."

"Actually, I need you to come with me. I have something to show you."

"I see." She waved her hands down at her sides. "Is casual okay?"

He hefted his shoulders and smiled. "Do you have a pair of jeans?"

"Jeans?" Those eyes rounded in surprise again. "Yes."

This was not going the way he'd planned. Not that he'd actually planned. He'd simply hopped in his car and followed his heart. *Heart*?

"Jared?" Eve's gaze narrowed with concern.

He must have been frowning at the sound of his own thoughts. This was most definitely not the way he'd wanting things to play out. For one thing, he hadn't expected an audience of half the Baron clan. Especially not supervised by the Governor himself. "If you wouldn't mind changing, I'll wait."

She nodded. "Give me ten."

As she ran up the stairs and he called after her. "Bring a hat too."

Looking over her shoulder at him, that frown was back. "Got it."

"Come have a seat while you wait." The Governor waved him toward an empty chair. Like good little soldiers, the puppies followed behind.

"Thank you." Jared sat and studied the faces of the men doing the same with him.

Chase was the first to speak up. "I understand y'all upgraded your rain system last year."

"That's right." He nodded. Thankful there were no questions about Eve. "In the knick of time too. We have quite a bit of captured water for filling the drinking troughs. The expense was high, but we'd be selling off cattle prematurely about now if not for the rainwater capture system."

"We've been thinking about doing that here." Mitch, the Senator, was the only person not looking at him as if he were a fox in the hen house. "If we don't get some rain soon, we're going to be selling off quite a chunk of the herd."

"If it'll help, I might be able to spare one of the tanks."

Mitch smiled. "Thanks. I'll let you know if it comes down to that."

Jared knew the Barons had used a rain water capture system for decades to fill the property ponds, but it wasn't quite as efficient as the new system he'd installed last year. "Any time."

The sound of boot heels clicking down wooden steps had him turning to see Eve hop off the last step and stand smiling at the bottom of the stairs. "Ready."

Pushing to his feet, he nodded at the Governor. "See you soon, sir."

A few heads nodded in return, a hand or two waved. One of the granddaughters, whose name he didn't remember, smiled at him. A nice smile. He could see the family resemblance, but it didn't have near the wattage that Eve's grin held.

Leading the way out the door, Eve trotted down the front steps. "So what's this all about?"

Jared held the car door open for her. "Working on the house yesterday got me thinking."

"Doesn't it always." She clicked her seat belt in place.

"Yeah. I can see that. Anyhow," he shifted into gear and headed for his place, "I think there's more that needs to be done than simply cutting a check."

"Agreed."

"I don't have any spare time, but nonetheless, I want to help."

She didn't say a word, but her smile grew a little wider.

"Obviously, there are a lot of veterans who need help with affordable housing. Especially special needs housing."

"I know. That's why I risk letting some crazy rich person name a major perfume something totally inappropriate. The egos of the very wealthy can be conducive to huge payouts for naming rights."

"Same for companies. I miss the old days when a ballpark was named for something that mattered to the town, not for the highest corporate bidder."

"I know what you mean. Makes me like Boston a little more than this Texas fan should."

That made him laugh. So the lady knew business, charity, cars, and now baseball. No one could be that perfect. There had to be something wrong with her.

"Earth to Jared."

"Oh, sorry. My mind wandered."

"I noticed." Thankfully, she was still smiling at him.

"One of the foremen at the construction site mentioned the high number of veterans applying for housing that they can't help. For many of the veterans, their biggest challenge to an ordinary life is dealing with PTSD."

Eve nodded. "It's crazy how we send off sweet, happy young men, and bring back too many broken and bent men with no hope for help."

"Like I said before, I'd like to help." He pulled into his own property, but rather than take the main drive to the house, he headed east onto the dirt road that led to the stables. "And I think I have an idea, but I want you to tell me what you think."

"Okay. Let me have it."

Two horses, saddled and ready, were tied to the wooden corral fence. Jared slowed the car and hopped out. "You do ride?"

Her gaze went from the horse to him. "Assuming you want to continue this conversation on horseback, it's a little late to be asking, don't you think?"

Oops. She had a point.

A bubble of sweet laughter erupted. "Don't look so aghast. Of course I know how to ride."

"You'll like Sugar. She's sweet and does exactly as told."

Eve scratched the large animal's jaw and murmured something he couldn't quite hear, but the horse's ear twitched, her lips moved, and her head dipped closer to Eve.

Whatever she'd told Sugar had made the horse happy. Suddenly, he found himself wishing she'd scratch under his chin and whisper sweet things into his ear. Wouldn't that be something?

CHAPTER SEVEN

E ve had no idea what all this was about, but any chance to get to know Jared better was fine with her. Even though she was positive that the teasing from her brothers could only escalate, she was also positive that he was worth it. And he was right, Sugar was a seriously easy to handle horse. They'd ridden away from the stables in silence and had just left the edge of all the ranching buildings when the soft hills of the property rolled out in front of them. "So what have you got in mind?"

"We've got a lot of land."

"You do. Texas is a big place."

"And I have a few horses that aren't always in use."

Now he had her interest piqued.

"Some are incredibly easy horses, like Sugar."

"I know you're going somewhere with this." Letting go of the reins with one hand, she patted the sweet horse lightly.

"I'd like to find a way to use my ranch to help the families of traumatized veterans. I know that equine therapy is popular for diagnosed disabilities, I also know that some of the kids are stressed by what's happened to their families. These kids aren't disabled themselves and don't qualify for special services, but their worlds are still upside down and the aftereffects can linger for years."

So far, he'd nailed one of the bigger loopholes in veteran care that she'd noticed through the years. And she liked where he was going with it.

"There are lots of programs for doing trail rides with kids. Mostly they consist of walking a line of horses, nose to tail, with little else along the way. A novelty for city kids, but far from the freeing experience a real ride can be."

Didn't she know that. As a kid they'd all learned how to saddle and care for their own horses and they'd enjoyed being tossed out the front door in the morning and spending the entire day riding the land. Up the hills, over the creeks, racing in the empty pastures, stopping to lunch with a packed picnic, and sometimes they'd tie up the horses and swim in the pond. It was a ton of fun and had helped every one of them a lot more than just learning to be responsible around horses. "Are you thinking free range trails, so-to-speak?"

He smiled at her. "Exactly. A morning or afternoon I think would be best. All day for kids who have never been on a horse may be a bit much. We'd have to do some simple horse instructions first. Basics."

"You'd need plenty of volunteers too. Can't just let kids run off on their own."

"Joys of liability. I figured we'd need some help but haven't a clue how many is wise."

The way he stared off into the distance, Eve could tell that in this short time he'd given the idea a great deal of thought and wished she better understood what had brought it on. The idea had a good deal of merit. It also sounded like a goodly amount of expense too. "There are some equestrian therapy centers who I can talk to. They might be able to give me some good advice. And maybe a good lawyer for this sort of thing." She'd donated time and money to charities but didn't have a clue about the legal side of any of it.

They'd come over a hill top by Texas standards and looked down on a massive pasture with a pond, a few scattered trees for shading the cattle, and the same creek that ran through Baron land.

"There." He pointed to the outrider shack that all ranches had scattered throughout the land for the hands to use in an emergency of some kind. "I thought we could convert that into a slightly more comfortable rest stop. Bathrooms. Kitchenette for hot chocolate in winter and cool drinks in summer."

"You could do an occasional camping night. Fire pit, S'mores, sleep under the stars, but with running water for toileting."

His head turned to look at her and a broad grin stretched from one side of his face to the other. "I like that." The same far-off twinkle of a short while ago reappeared.

"It's a good idea. Running water just makes it a little nicer." She shifted in her saddle. "May I ask how you came up with it?"

His gaze lingered in the distance a little longer than she'd expected, then he leaned one hand heavily on the saddle's horn and faced her. "Long story short, I was ten when my grandparents died. Nothing helped the hurt as much as the land and the horses. If sharing this with others can help, then I'm all for it. I just wasn't sure if the idea might be overly ambitious of me. I know the project will be a huge undertaking with some up-front costs."

"More like a lot." No point in not being realistic.

His smile didn't fade. "Yes. A lot. And there will be obstacles. But the more it mulls over in the back of my mind, the more I'm convinced it's doable. And even though I can't be hands on *and* run the ranch, it's better than just cutting a check."

No matter how many times she rode out on their own land, no matter how many beautiful places she traveled to, nothing took away the sense of wonder and home that warmed her at the sight of Texas hills. Especially during blue bonnet season. A few hours ago, she'd already begun to consider there was more to Jared Gold than the carousing pal of her jet-setting brother. Now she was absolutely positive there was so much more to this man. "I want to help."

Jared's head whipped around to face her. "You do?"

She could feel her cheeks pulling at her lips. "Don't look so surprised. I really do." One more charity wasn't going to kill her. At least she didn't think so. Then again, she let her gaze drift to Jared. Of course, having a hunk heading up the next charity wasn't such a bad thing either.

From his pocket, his cell phone sounded. It took her a

few moments, but she finally recognized the ring-tone as "Friends in Low Places" and couldn't hold back the laugh.

Jared rolled his eyes at her and muttered, "I like Garth Brooks," before answering. "Hello."

She couldn't hear the person on the other side, but from the deep frown cutting into his forehead, she didn't need to hear to know it wasn't anything good.

Nothing could send a heart rate racing more than hearing your mother prattling on frantically in a clear and obvious state of panic. "Mom. Slow down. What happened?"

"Mary. Oh dear God, I don't think she's breathing. There's no one here."

"Mom. Deep breath. Cook went to the store. She'll be home soon. What happened to Mary?"

"I. Don't. Know. She's just lying on the floor. Father, help her. I think she fell down the stairs."

"Crap." He was too far from the house to help. "Did you call 911?"

"What good will that do? This isn't Houston."

"Mom. Hang up. Call 911 now. Hold tight. Don't move her. I'm on my way." Jared wanted to turn the horse around and haul ass back to the house, but he needed to make a call first.

He looked to Eve, whose eyes held all the worry he felt. "Mary took a fall. She's unconscious."

All she did was nod and turn the horse without needing any more information. She was in hurry up mode too, except he needed to make one more call.

Flipping through contacts, he hit the Governor's number and loosening the reins, nudged the horse into a full gallop.

"Hello."

"Governor. This is Jared."

"You sound out of breath, boy. What's wrong? Eve?"

"Sorry. No. We're racing back to my house. Mary took

a fall. She's unconscious at the bottom of the stairs and Mom is freaking out."

"No worries. I'll call Doc Rayburn. Have him meet us there."

"Thanks, sir." He didn't bother with anymore pleasantries. There was no need for more information. It was clear with the word "us" that the Governor would beat them all home. Knowing the family the way Jared did, he expected to find Ms. Lila there as well.

He and Eve were flying back. Sugar was a sweet horse and thank heavens she was also fast as lightning. His horse too. As a matter of fact, he was pretty sure the two animals were enjoying the chance to let loose. He just hoped his mother didn't have a heart attack before the cavalry arrived.

Usually, the return trip home always seemed shorter than the trip leaving home. Every party, every long drive, even though the distance and time was the same, it always felt shorter going home. Not this time. The ride seemed eternal. If memory served correctly, he hadn't raced a horse since he was a teen. He and his buddies would race like their very lives depended on it and then his dad would scold them for over-working the horses. They'd loved every minute of it. Right now, he wished his horse really could fly.

By the time the house was within sight, he could see the row of cars as well. The Governor had no doubt come with reinforcements. The sight had him and Eve pushing their horses a little harder than they probably should have. Neither stopped at the stables, they raced right up to the back door. Eve was first off her mount. "I'll walk them back to the stables. You go see what's going on. I'll meet you."

He shook his head, nearly jumped off the horse and was already speed dialing the stable. "No need. I'll have Randy come get them."

"Okay." She followed him into the house running almost as fast as he was.

Before he got through the kitchen, he'd briefed Randy and was once again praying nothing was serious with Mary.

Doc Rayburn was standing beside Mary on a gurney

and the EMTs were about to wheel her out the door. Jared's first thought was if they weren't care flighting her, then she couldn't be too serious. Only the oxygen mask gave him pause. "How is she, doc?"

The older man who had been caring for their family since before he was born sighed. "We'll run some tests at the hospital, but she's still unconscious."

"That's not good, is it?" He didn't need a medical degree to know the longer you were out the more serious the prognosis.

"Depends." Doc pressed his lips tightly together then laid a hand on his forearm. "I gave your mother a light sedative. She's pretty shook up. You check on her and I'll let you know as soon as we have more info on Mary."

He bobbed his head and hurrying after the gurney in the front doorway, took hold of Mary's chilled hand. "Don't you worry about Jake. I'll take care of him till you get back. But you'd better hurry and get well fast. I don't want to make my own bed."

The doc chuckled as the EMTs carried her the rest of the way to the truck. "If she heard you, that should get her up." He patted Jared on the back. "I'm going to head to the hospital myself. I'll let you know when we know more."

"Thanks." Jared extended his hand to shake the doc's and then let his gaze follow the ambulance down the driveway. Standing frozen in place, his mind fixated on Mary's pale face. He'd been concerned by the frantic tone in his mother's voice, but seeing their beloved housekeeper so fragile and pasty and out cold, he understood where the fear had come from. He simply couldn't imagine their home without Mary around.

"Your mom is in the parlor with my grandparents." The slight touch on his arm reminded him he wasn't alone. "Do you want us to leave?"

"No!" The single word came out more harshly than he'd intended. "No. Thank you. I think... Mom would appreciate the company."

Eve's head tipped up and down slowly, but her expression seemed almost as lost as he felt.

"And so would I." They'd only spent a few days together, but if he'd learned one thing in all his years of bachelorhood, it was that hiding behind bravado got him nowhere. Fast.

Eve pushed up on her tippy toes and kissed him on the cheek. "I'll stay as long as you need me." Patting his arm again, she turned and walked to the parlor while he resisted the urge to lift his hand and touch his cheek where her lips had been.

"She's feeling better." The Governor sat beside his wife.

His mom was on the other side of Lila Baron. "She looked so still."

"It will be all right. Doc Rayburn is wonderful." Lila patted his mother's hand. "You'll see."

Eve looked from the three people on the large sofa over her shoulder toward the hall. A slight frown descended over her brows. "Doesn't Mary have a grandson?"

"Oh." His mother gasped. "What are we going to tell little Jake?"

"Nothing yet." Jared walked to the bar and poured his mom more water. "He's at camp till the end of the week. By then I'm sure Mary will be fine." At least he hoped so. Mary was the only family the little boy had.

His mom nodded. "You're right. Thank heavens this was camp week. I can't imagine how scared that poor little boy would have been if he'd found his Grammy on the floor like that. I'm not blaming God for Mary's fall, but you know he's got a hand in protecting everyone."

All heads in the room bobbed in agreement. Jared looked at his watch, wondering how long before he'd have any news.

"I put in a call to the chief of staff at the hospital. The second they know anything, we'll know." The Governor seemed to be reading his mind. "If you want to head over and see to it that all is well, we'll stay here with your mother."

"No." His mom shook her head. "I'm feeling rather sleepy. The pills the doctor gave me must be kicking in. I'll just go home before I fall asleep."

"Nonsense." Ms. Lila patted her hand again. "The Governor and I will take you home. Explain to your husband what's happened."

The second his mother nodded her approval, he knew just how shook up she'd been. Like Ms Lila, under normal circumstances his mom was a force to be reckoned with. Right now, for the first time, he realized she wasn't getting any younger. "I'll head to the hospital. See what I can find out."

"That will be good," his mom muttered, the sedative kicking in more heavily.

The Governor walked up to him. "Don't worry about her. Keep us posted. And Jared…"

"Yes?"

"Anything you need, anything at all, you know how to find us."

Jared nodded. "Thanks. Appreciate it." The Barons and Golds had been neighbors since before he was born. Living in ranch country wasn't the same as the suburbs. When a motor vehicle was needed to get from ranch to ranch, there were no pick-up games of stickball in the street, or running back and forth to the homes of all the kids on the block. There were no blocks in ranch country. Even though growing up he'd hardly ever visited the Barons, that didn't change the fact that neighbors could always be counted on in a pinch. His grandfather spoke highly of Ms. Lila's father. No one in this ranching community had cared for a military man taking over Lila's family ranch, but as the years passed, the Governor won over every last person within a hundred-mile radius, including the Gold family. Once Jared had been put in charge of Golden Creek and gotten to know the Governor, rancher to rancher, he understood exactly why the man was revered.

"Do you want company?" Eve followed behind everyone.

As much as he really wanted her with him, more than he would have expected, it wasn't fair to her. "Thanks, but no. I have no idea what's going on, but experience tells me I could be waiting for news for hours."

"All the more reason for someone to be with you."

Her determination made him smile. "Thanks, but no. I can handle this on my own."

"You sure?"

He shrugged. "No, but we'll find out."

A soft chuckle escaped, followed by a sweet smile.

Jared came within inches of changing his mind, quietly reminding himself it wasn't fair to make Eve wait this out. He pulled the door shut behind him, glanced up at the expansive Texas sky and said a small prayer. An image of little Jake years ago intently playing on the parlor rug for hours with an old train set Jared had found in the attic while his grandmother worked, made him smile. For that little boy's sake, Mary had better be up and about, and soon.

CHAPTER EIGHT

Ten fifteen in the morning. Even though Eve's only interaction with Mary had been mostly from church, she liked the woman and felt awful for her and her little grandson. After tossing and turning for hours, unable to stop thinking about Mary's fall, young Jake, and the toll all of this could take on Jared, Eve finally gave up and decided heading into work early would be the best distraction. Tinkering with a new scent would be perfect for idle hands, except three hours later, Jared heavy on her mind, she had little to show for it.

"I sure hope it's a man who has you this distracted." Isabel stood over Eve's shoulder.

How long had her assistant stood there unnoticed? Dang, Eve was going to have to get her act together this morning. "It's not a man on my mind." At least not the way Isabel meant.

"Too bad." The young woman sighed heavily and shook her head. "But something has you off your game."

"My game is just fine. I'm worried about a neighbor."

"Fine, huh?" Isabel lifted her chin in the direction of the latest concoction Eve had been trying unsuccessfully to focus on.

Eve looked down at her work. "What?"

"Had you been paying attention, you would have noticed that this is the third time you've dropped MOC into that mixture."

Brows dipping into a frown, Eve held up the tube of ingredients. Had she really added too much Methyl Octine Carbonate?

"You keep adding that and that lovely hint of a violet

scent you're going for is going to smell like a cucumber salad."

Letting her hands drop to the table, Eve leaned back. "I should have just stayed in bed."

"That bad?" Her assistant set a tall cup of coffee in front of her and slid onto the stool beside her. "I added a little Louisiana chicory. You'll like it."

The aroma rising from the cup was enough to cheer any coffee lover's spirits. Eve took a short sip and almost groaned with satisfaction. "You've been holding out on me."

"Nah," Isabel shook her head, "my cousin Marvin brought me some this weekend after a visit to New Orleans. I was going to share even if you weren't screwing up."

Normally, Eve would have shot back a snappy retort, but she really was distracted, by Mary's accident, Mrs. Gold's near breakdown, the fate of little Jake, and how deep under her skin Jared had settled in after only a few days. She glanced at her phone on the counter beside her. There was no reason for her to be kept in the loop; still, she'd hoped Jared would find a minute to give her an update, but even more, she really wanted to hear Jared's voice. Another thing that had her wondering what the heck was going on.

Like the scents she created that lingered in the air and in a person's memory, Jared was entrenched in the very fiber of her being practically from the minute he startled her into dumping caviar all over herself. Not since Bradley Roman had moved to town in sixth grade and been seated at the desk in front of her had she been so continually flustered by a member of the opposite sex.

"Want to tell me about it?" Cradling the mug in her hands, Isabel blew at the coffee.

It took Eve a second to bring her thoughts back around to the conversation with Isabel. "The ranch house neighbor has had the same housekeeper for decades."

Isabel nodded, waiting for more.

"Yesterday she took a tumble and knocked herself out. At least that's what we thought. Turns out she has a ruptured aneurysm."

"Whoa," Isabel whistled. "That doesn't sound good."

"Nope. The doctors say we should find some reassurance that the rupture didn't kill her. Apparently, that's more common than I want to consider at this point. Still, they had to do emergency surgery."

"Oh, man." Isabel whistled again.

"The doctors say the recovery time could be as little as a month or, depending on damage, years. We're supposed to know more today. I'm waiting for an update." Eve's gaze once again darted to her quiet phone.

"Does the housekeeper have any family?"

"That's the rub. She has a nine-year-old grandson completely dependant on her."

Isabel blew out a deep sigh and frowned. "I really am sorry. Now I really wish it had just been a man setting you off kilter."

No point in mentioning that a man very much had something to do with her being off kilter.

"I guess I'll give you a pass on the mistakes. Do you want to just go home for the day? I mean, before we wind up wasting perfectly good chemicals?"

"I can't. I really do need to get some work done."

Isabel shook her head. "Go home. And once we know the housekeeper is going to be all right—because I refuse to accept otherwise—then may I strongly suggest you go find yourself a man? Really."

"You're incorrigible." The running tease brought a smile to Eve's lips. "Don't ever change."

"Deal." Isabel hopped up from the stool and headed back to her own work.

Standing, Eve picked up the uncooperative phone. Fingers clenched around the device, the cell rang. Jared's number appeared on the screen. "Hello."

"Hey, sorry I didn't get back to you sooner. It's been a madhouse here."

"Things that crazy at the hospital?"

"I'm not at the hospital. I finally heard from the doctors. They're pleased Mary made it through the night."

Eve sighed. She hadn't realized that Mary's condition

post surgery had been that precarious.

"They're going to keep her in an induced coma for her brain to heal and the swelling to dissipate. Initial testing shows some delayed response on her left side, but they assure me not till the swelling decreases and they're sure there won't be any more brain bleeds will they know how long her recovery will be."

"Brain bleeds?"

"Yeah. The doctor prattled on a bunch of words I'm unfamiliar with, but he says the next few days will determine a lot."

Eve supposed that waiting a few days was better than the alternative if Mary hadn't survived the night.

"My mother is at the hospital with her now so she's not alone. Your grandmother is going to spell my mom after lunch. I think the church is signing up people to take turns sitting with her."

"Good idea. I might pop over too." Heaven knew she wasn't doing anyone any good at work. "If you're not at the hospital then what else has you running crazy?"

"If you mean besides the second-floor a/c crapping out, and blowing a hydraulic line in the middle of unloading a few hundred pounds of feed, I have a heifer struggling with a delivery. I'm waiting on the vet now."

"Oh, no."

"Yeah. A lot of times these things work themselves out, but not always. All I can do is all I can do. Blast. Randy is flagging me down. I have to run. I'll call later."

She didn't get a chance to say anything as the line went dead. All she needed was one more thing to worry about. Poor mama cow.

"I know, girl." Jared ran his hand down the young heifer's nose. Some days he wished he could just pull the covers over his head and stay in bed. All morning he'd been putting out one fire after the other. One thing was pretty clear, whatever progress Mary made, it wouldn't be in time to have her home for her grandson's return from camp.

All of which meant he had some fast thinking to do about caring for Jake.

"Hey there." The soft voice that wafted across the old barn was an instant balm to his troubled thoughts.

Lifting his attention from the struggling heifer, Eve stood in the doorway, something in her hands. Backlit in sunlight, she looked like an angel straight from heaven.

"I thought you might be hungry." She held up a thermal bag in each hand. "I'd love to say I made it all myself, but then you wouldn't want to eat any of it."

"This is a nice surprise." He couldn't have stopped the bright smile that took over his face if he wanted to. "Not complaining, but shouldn't you be working?"

"Yes." She set the bags down. "But I wasn't getting much done. Too distracted. Besides, what good is it to be the boss if I can't come and go as I please?"

"Good point." He reached for the bags. "What have we got here?"

"I looked for food easy to eat in a barn."

That made him chuckle. "I didn't realize there was such a thing as barn cuisine."

"There is now." Eve waved at one bag. "That's got cool drinks in it. I figured you wouldn't want wine or beer while working."

He nodded. "Good call."

"If you want warm, there's fried chicken and meatballs and corn on the cob. If you want cold, there's a Reuben sandwich, an Italian combo, and a small cheese platter. Oh, and baked potato chips. Both regular and mesquite barbecue."

If the old adage *the way to a man's heart was through his stomach* was true, then Eve Baron had his heart completely wrapped around her little finger. "Wow."

The way her smile bloomed at his reaction gave his heart an extra kick. He really did like seeing her smile, but more so, he liked knowing he was the one who put the smile on her face in the first place. He liked it a lot. Way more than he should. As a matter of fact, he'd like to be around to make her smile like that all the time. "Are you free for dinner tonight?"

Her eyes widened. "We haven't even had lunch and you're already thinking dinner?"

"I'm a growing boy." He carried the bags to just outside the stall where the cow was being kept. "Let me get us a small table."

"No need." She pulled an old quilt out of her backpack. "This way you can stay close to mama."

"A woman who thinks of everything." It only took a few minutes to spread the blanket out on some clean hay and settle themselves in for a picnic lunch.

Legs crossed, Eve sat in front of him, pulling out napkins, paper plates, and plastic cutlery. "I didn't know which you'd prefer so I figured a little of everything was easiest."

"It all looks delicious." He reached for a piece of fried chicken and a meatball. "What do you say we cut the sandwiches in half then we can each have both."

The way one eyebrow shot up high on her forehead, anyone would think he'd suggested a game of strip poker after lunch. "I've been told I have a healthy appetite, but not that healthy."

Great job. Open mouth, insert foot. "All I meant was—"

She smiled and raised her hand. "I know what you meant. I'm just used to sparring with brothers who love to tease."

All he did was nod. He was afraid anything he said might work against him. Instead, he took a bite of his chicken and tried not to dribble crisp fried crumbles. "This is great. I think it's better than Mary's. Where did you get it?"

"That smokehouse off the freeway. They have everything from frozen venison to hand dipped caramel apples. I really should stop in more often."

He was going to have to make note to do the same next time he needed a quick bite while on the road.

"So what's the story with mama cow?"

"First time mama. Labor stalled. The vet gave her a shot to move things along but had an emergency across the county he had to get to. He promises me there's room enough in her pelvis to deliver, so now it's just wait and watch."

"Poor thing must be so confused." She broke off a piece of bread from the end of the Italian combo sandwich and popped it into her mouth.

"First baby is always more work for mom."

"Ain't that the truth. One of my best friends from college had her first baby last year. Thirty-two hours in labor. Talk about a labor of love."

"My mother has never let me forget that she was in labor with me for three days." He reached for a napkin. "That particular memory is often brought up when my plans don't quite align with Mom's."

"Oh, I bet." She giggled. "If I'd been in labor with you for three days, I'd remind you at every cross word."

"And don't think Mom didn't do just that." Truth was, he loved his mother to death and was more than willing to bend over backwards for her. Just then the cow let out a long slow bellow.

"You tell him, girl." Eve laughed at the cow's timing as though she were reinforcing the concept of be good to your mamas.

"You never did tell me if you wanted to join me for dinner?" Hoping he didn't sound too eager, he took a bite of the Reuben to stop him from rambling on foolishly.

"I didn't?" Following suit, she took a bite of her sandwich, eyeing him through thick lush lashes. She slowly nodded. "That would be nice."

Nice was good. Better than no. Nodding, he smiled at her and resisted the urge to do a fist pump or victory jig. But he did have to deal with Mary and Jake. "I may not have a whole lot of free time after Jake comes home." The whole idea of needing to do right by Mary's grandson continued to linger in the back of his every thought.

The sandwich halfway to Eve's mouth, she let her hands lower to her lap without taking a bite. "What's going to happen to him?"

"Of course, he'll stay here. I have no idea if Mary made plans if anything happened to her, but even though they live in the quarters over the garage, the ranch is still the only home Jake remembers. I'm not going to pull that out from under him too."

She shook her head. "No, you can't do that." For a few long quiet moments, she stared down at the half-eaten sandwich before her gaze lifted to meet his. "If you need anything at all, you know, with Jake, don't hesitate to ask."

"Thanks. I just may have to take you up on that." Considering he hardly spent any time with the boy, with any boy, if Mary's recovery dragged on, he might be needing a lot of help. The next bite of lunch almost caught in his throat. From where he stood, the sandwich wasn't the only thing that he'd bitten off more than he could chew.

CHAPTER NINE

The week was long and tiring. She'd looked forward to every opportunity to spend time with Jared. To get to know him better. The only challenge was it took days for Eve to get her concentration back. Right now, there was nothing she wanted more than to escape the city and regroup on the ranch. Having Jared nearby was the icing on the cake. She resisted the urge to call him from the road and turned down the Baron driveway.

Slamming the car door shut behind her, she took in a deep breath. Even this close to Houston, the air was just different. Some of it was less traffic, some of it was fewer people, a lot of it was fewer housing developments, but most of it was probably the love and comfort that came from acres upon acres of rolling hills and family love.

Gravel crunched under approaching tires. Her heart lifted at the prospect that maybe it was Jared coming to see her, which made no sense at all. It was barely the end of the normal work day. Why would Jared be coming over when they'd agreed to meet for supper in a couple of hours?

The familiar car came to a stop beside hers. Craig climbed out and slammed the door shut behind him.

"Well, isn't this a nice surprise. I thought you were working on a film in New Mexico or Arizona. One of those states."

Coming up next to her, he kissed her cheek and slung an arm over her shoulder as they walked step by step into the house. "I just flew back. Everything is rolling fine. Permits won't allow shooting over the weekend, so given the choice of coming home or hanging out in a motel in the middle of nowhere New Mexico, I opted for the ranch."

"Grams will love that. She's happiest when all the grand-chicks come home to roost."

Craig barked out a short laugh. "That she is. Besides, I promised to help finish that new length of fencing going in to keep the bulls in."

"I wondered who was making all the commotion outside," the Governor called out from behind his desk, waving Eve over. "I know you and Jared had plans to go out to dinner, but when I was talking to him today about Mary's condition, he mentioned in passing the idea of a non-profit trail ride for potentially troubled kids. Your grandmother and I like the idea. We'd like to discuss it more, so I suggested he join the family for dinner."

Join the family for dinner. The words echoed in her head. She wasn't so sure she was ready to share Jared just yet with so many of her family. The teasing was all well and good with the people closest to her, but she was hesitant to bring Jared into the mix. Personally. To be scared off. *Scared off.* The thought of chasing him away before she'd had time to cement what the relationship possibilities were literally made her heart hurt. All of this week, chatting on the phone every day, sometimes more than once, she didn't want to think about going back to a life of eat, sleep, work, with only sporadic social interactions that didn't involve a charity gala. Looking forward to curling up on the sofa and chatting with Jared had quickly become the highlight of her day.

"There's lemonade in the parlor." Her grandmother stuck her head in the office door. "It will be a small group for dinner."

Small was good. Fewer people to pick on her and Jared.

"If y'all will excuse me, I want to go shower off the New Mexico dust before supper." Craig leaned in and kissed his grandmother on the cheek on his way out the door.

Her grandfather pushed to his feet, reached for the cane he didn't really need, and with Moon at his heels, followed his wife into the parlor. "This Jared has a good head on his shoulders. Thought his father had lost his mind turning over an operation that size to his son, but it's worked out well."

Eve slowed her steps. She knew what was coming. This was her grandfather in matchmaker mode.

"Man like that knows how to handle responsibilities, challenges and opportunities. Knows not to let them slip through his fingers."

Any minute now, she knew the words husband and father and her name were about to be linked.

"Why, some of your own cousins wouldn't have been able to take on such a responsibility. And now, to want to share that with underprivileged kids of the men and women who served and sacrificed for this country, well, I couldn't be prouder of him if he were a Baron."

She was pretty proud of him too. The way he'd taken point to make sure Mary was getting the best possible care and keeping tabs on her grandson at camp. The gentle way he talked the heifer through her discomfort until she delivered a healthy baby melted Eve's heart. She loved so many things about him, but his caring heart was most definitely at the top of the list.

"No idea why some smart, beautiful, and kind woman," the old man actually stood by his favorite chair, and rather than sit, stared her down, "hasn't snatched him up and walked him down the aisle."

"Men don't walk down the aisle." It was a dumb response, but it was what popped into mind. No matter how much she loved Jared, she was not going to let her grandfather rush her down the...*loved Jared?* Her mouth ran dry and her brain stuttered. Of course, she loved Jared. He was a good man. A good neighbor. And had become a good friend. She loved all her friends, and her family. She did. But who was she kidding? She didn't sit on the edge of her seat waiting for a phone call from her grandmother or her best buddies.

Holy matrimony, she'd gone and fallen in love with Jared Gold.

★

Somehow, when it came to the Governor, Jared felt as though an invitation to dinner were the same thing as being summoned to the principal's office. The bright side of the invitation was that it included Eve. This last week of having her in his life to talk to and bounce ideas and problems off of had made even the most disruptive elements of his daily challenges much more palatable.

Pulling into the front drive of the Baron house, he stepped out of the jeep, slapped his hat against his leg out of sheer habit, and sucking in a deep breath, marched up the stairs. Anyone would think he was on death's row and not about to have a nice family dinner with the lady in his life. Of course, this being the first time dining with the Barons as... as what? Eve's friend? Eve's boyfriend? Eve's intended? *Intended*. Now wasn't that an old-fashioned word. Where it popped out from, he had no idea, but like a bolt of lightning, it struck him clear as day. He most definitely had intentions when it came to Eve. He just hadn't put them into words yet. But with everything going on, he wasn't so sure now was a good time to blurt out that he didn't want to be friends, and he most definitely wanted to be more than a casual date.

As had happened the last few times he'd come to visit, the front door opened before he could ring the bell. This time, it was Eve's brother Craig filling the doorway. "Saw you coming up the steps. Thought I'd save you the trouble of over taxing that arm by ringing the doorbell."

"Appreciate it." He flashed a smile that he hoped conveyed a confidence he wasn't so sure he felt. Not that confidence was a problem for him. Normally he was the guy that walked into a room like he owned the place, knowing no one would question whether or not he did. But when it came to Eve, he'd found his confidence slipping ever so slightly. He couldn't afford a single misstep around her. Or around her brothers. He did not want to lose this girl. More than anything in this world, he wanted to keep Eve in his life. And wasn't that an interesting revelation.

"Welcome." Lila Baron smiled at him from her favorite chair. The growing puppies snoozed soundly in their designated beds. "Come sit."

He followed his neighbor's gesture and took a seat on the sofa.

"It's a small gathering for dinner tonight," his hostess pointed out. "More intimate that way, don't you think?"

Was this a trick question? Not sure, he nodded and hoped he hadn't failed.

"My cousin Colton was going to pop in, but he ran into some last-minute complications on a project." Craig poured himself a drink and lifted the glass in Jared's direction. "Would you like a cocktail before dinner?"

"I'll have whatever you're having."

Craig bobbed his head and Jared had the strangest feeling that his evening was going to be filled with tests. That or he was becoming strangely paranoid. Speaking of paranoid, he casually glanced around the large room and out the doorway to the hall. Had Eve bailed on the dinner and left him to fend for himself with her family?

"She'll be down in a minute." The Governor clearly had a gift at reading minds. Jared was going to have to be more careful around the retired Marine. "What's the latest word on Mary?"

"Promising. The doctors are hopeful, but no matter what, even assuming she has no permanent impairment, she could be looking at a long recovery time. If there's some loss of function, she could need to go to rehab before coming home."

"And when do they think that will be?"

He blew out the same deep sigh he'd exhaled when the doctor had told him not to expect Mary home for at least another month. The words still had him a little rattled.

"Hello." Eve came through the doorway.

The second he heard her voice, he sprang to his feet. His mother had made sure that standing when a lady entered the room came as naturally as breathing. If he didn't do so, he just knew somehow his mother would find out and no matter how far away she might be, the woman would magically appear beside him to poke him in the rib cage. The next instinct was to reach for Eve's hand, kiss her lightly and make sure she sat beside him. The problem with that scenario was whether or not the men in the room would consider that grounds to have him run out of town on the proverbial rail. He settled for smiling and muttering a barely audible, "Hi."

"Dinner isn't ready yet." Ms. Lila gestured toward the sofa. "Might as well take our seats again."

"We were just discussing Mary's prognosis." The Governor, who had remained seated, tapped his wedding ring on the head of his cane. "When does the boy come home?"

And that was the latest tidbit he'd been wrestling with and was hoping to talk with Eve about this evening. "Camp officially ends Saturday, but the parents won't be bringing the kids home till Sunday."

Eve's eyes widened. "That's just two more days?"

"Yeah." His head dipped once and he swallowed hard. "I freely admit, it's a little unsettling."

Ms. Lila smiled. "Not much experience with children?"

He shook his head. "It's not like Jake and I are strangers, but the ranch keeps me pretty busy. Our paths don't cross very often." To his surprise, without looking at him, Eve reached over and covering his hand with hers, offered a reassuring squeeze. Grateful for the support, he weaved his fingers with hers and held on tight.

"We'll work something out." Eve squeezed his hand again.

The word *we'll* had his chest swelling with something akin to relief wrapped in joy. The idea that she was willing to be a part of we instantly took some of the pressure of how to care for Mary's grandson off his shoulders, while simultaneously making him want to kick up his heels.

"Have you decided where he'll stay?" Eve asked.

"Doesn't Mary live in the quarters over the garage?" Lila Baron seemed to be thinking something through.

Jared nodded. He'd been thinking it through too but hadn't come to a decision on if it made more sense for him to move into Mary's quarters, or for Jake to move into the main house. At least in the main house he had other staff to help him keep tabs on the boy while Jared was working.

"What are you thinking?" This time Eve let her gaze level with his.

"Sleeping arrangements."

"Care to get more specific?" The corners of her mouth tipped upward and he had a feeling it had nothing to do with where to house Mary's grandson.

"I think it would be easier on me if he stayed at the house, but I'm not convinced it's what's best for Jake."

"Does the boy spend much time at your house?" Ms. Lila asked.

Jared shrugged. "He spends a lot of time in the kitchen. He does his homework there. Sometimes he helps the cook if Mary's really busy. But I rarely see him in the main part of the house."

"How rarely is rarely?" The Governor sported a stern expression.

"A handful of times a year. Most often around holidays when Mary is decorating for seasonal festivities."

"Then I guess that answers your question." Ms. Lila both grinned and dipped her chin as if that was that. Too bad he wasn't sure what his answer was.

"Good. Now that it's settled that the boy will be staying with you, I'd like to discuss your charity."

What Jared didn't understand is why did he seem to be the only person in the room who didn't see the answer so clearly? At least, in a roundabout way, he now knew that Jake was moving into a guest room. Preferably near him. Just in case. "Yes, sir."

"I've discussed your idea with Mrs. Baron."

Jared nodded. He had no idea where the Governor was going with this and didn't want to give his confusion away by saying something stupid.

"We like it very much."

That was good news. Not that it would change anything if the Governor thought it was a bad idea, but his negative impression would give him pause.

"It's a big job starting a charity organization of the caliber you're thinking about. Especially now with the added distraction of caring for a young boy."

This time he probably nodded a bit more vehemently than he had a moment ago. He expected just about everything was going to be more challenging while Jake was his responsibility.

"Lila and I have the experience with this sort of thing and most definitely more time than you do."

There was no arguing that. The Barons were founding members of many a South Texas charity.

"Start up costs are going to be high because of the caliber of horse needed. Legal fees, and any construction won't be cheap."

"I imagine not." Finally something he could say.

"My wife and I want to partner with you."

"Excuse me?" Of all the things he expected the Governor to say, that wasn't even remotely on his list of possibilities.

"There'll be a need for more horses. The right horses. Some extra hands. And there will be a need for sponsors. We can help defer some of the up-front costs, and then reach out to others to off set the rest of the expenses. What do you say?"

As distracted as he'd been all week with Mary's health and worrying about her grandson, the idea of the charity for kids of wounded veterans who were falling through the cracks wouldn't let go of him. Deep down, he knew he needed to move forward. The days of simply writing a check were now gone. He had no doubt that the idea was a good one, and that he and his family ranch had what it would take to make the idea work. Except, the one key thing he didn't have a whole lot of under normal circumstances, and even less of now—time. Regardless, there was no one he trusted more than the Barons to help him get this idea off the ground. "Where do I sign?"

Both the Governor and his wife laughed. Eve simply held onto his hand, and yet, it was more reassuring than anything the doctors or Governor had said to him. Staring down at her long beautiful fingers and soft delicate hand, he was certain of one thing, Eve Baron was the best thing to happen to him. It didn't matter if they'd been growing closer for one week or one month or one year. However long, he was most definitely falling in love with this sweet, kindhearted woman. The question at hand now was how could he win her over? He couldn't go back to living without Eve in his life. He just couldn't.

CHAPTER TEN

After dinner Friday night, the conversation drifted around the new charity Jared wanted to start. No surprise to anyone, Eve's grandparents knew a great deal. The two had brought up several issues that hadn't occurred to Jared, and certainly hadn't occurred to her. By the time the rancher left the rambling home, he had a to-do list longer than his arm and she was thrilled that her family could be of help to him.

On Saturday morning the four of them had toured the land and facilities that Jared wanted to dedicate for the use of the charity. The Governor didn't believe in putting off for tomorrow what could be done today. Even if that meant calling a lawyer on his day off. By dinnertime, they had an appointment with the best non-profit attorney in the state, had a list of the best breeders and trainers, and by dessert had narrowed the list of horse breeders down to one. Connor Farraday. Apparently, the man knew horses the way she knew perfume. Maybe more. Another phone call from the Governor and he and Jared would be expected in West Texas the following weekend.

"It's pretty amazing how fast your grandfather can pull things together." Jared whizzed around a slow poke on the freeway who had yet to read a single sign that reminded drivers the left lane was for passing only.

"If I had a nickel for every time the Governor spouted the old adage, *it's not what you know but who you know*, I'd be a very rich lady."

"Sorry to point this out," Jared smiled at her, "but you already are a very rich lady."

She shrugged. "Okay, more rich. Between all his

connections, and his tendency to run every project he was involved with the same way he ordered around his troops, I have no doubt this new charity will shine sooner than later."

"Agreed." Jared shifted gears. "I know I've already said this, but it merits mentioning again. Thank you for coming with me today."

When the evening and plan making was finally over, she'd politely offered to go with Jared today to pick up Mary's grandson. To her surprise, Jared had taken her up on the offer before she'd even finished her sentence. So now, instead of heading to church with the family this Sunday morning, she was on her way to the other side of Hill Country to accompany Jared in his task of retrieving little Jake.

"Penny for your thoughts?" Jared barely glanced in her direction.

"Not worth that much." Smiling around her grandfather's neighbor was easier than she might have imagined.

"I doubt that." He kept his gaze on the road ahead.

"Back at you."

He blew out a deep sigh.

"By the time we get back to the ranch with Jake, we'll still have the better part of the afternoon ahead of us and frankly, I'm not sure what to do with him. Especially if he's upset about his grandmother, which I expect will be the case."

"Don't know about that."

"What to do with him or how upset he'll be?"

"I don't know a huge amount about kids, but I do remember a thing or two about both my half sisters. One of those things is that at Jake's age, kids still have unwavering faith in whatever adults tell them. If you tell him everything will be all right, that his grandmother will be home soon, he'll believe you."

"And if she doesn't come home soon? Then he'll never believe me again."

This time she blew out the sigh. "I suppose the doctor's optimism will have to be carefully portrayed, but if we go about life as normally as possible, so will he.”

Jared tipped his head to one side. “I sure do hope you’re right, but that still leaves me wondering what we’re going to do with him this afternoon.”

“Well.” One side of her face scrunched up. “This may be overkill, and I have no idea how Jake feels about water.”

He shrugged. “Neither do I. What are you thinking?”

“Kyle is in town. This is an off weekend for racing.”

Jared nodded, but kept his silence.

“Some of the family is going to spend the day on the *Baroness*. A kid might find it fun.”

The idea had possibilities. The few interactions he’d had with Jake replayed in the back of his mind as Jared tried to determine if boating was something the boy would enjoy. It was a bit of a shock to realize that for the most part the kid just stared at him and he’d made little effort to engage the boy. He really didn’t have a clue if Jake enjoyed outdoor activities or not. On the other hand, what did it matter? At least on the yacht, he’d have adult help. “I suppose we can ask him?”

Eve smiled. “I suppose we can.”

The twinkle in her eyes he’d grown so fond of told him she was politely teasing him. “Ask him we shall.”

Her head bobbed and he hoped that bringing Jake home was going to be as easy as being with Eve. Despite the miserable circumstances surrounding Mary, he wanted to believe that Eve’s analysis of the situation would be correct. He also wanted Mary to get well sooner than later and he really wanted the Barons help making everything right. Including finding a way to make Eve feel for him what he felt for her. A tall order as he saw it. Maybe it was time he said a few extra prayers during the rest of the drive, because right now the two things he wanted most in this world, bringing a healthy Mary home from the hospital and making Eve Baron a permanent part of his life, seemed pretty dang far out of his reach.

★

"Relax." Eve's brother Kyle handed her an iced tea. "Craig may occasionally be an overbearing—"

"I never said that." And she never would. At least not to his face. But Kyle was right, working more often than not with overly confident Hollywood types brought out her brother's pricklier side. Thankfully a few days grounded in Texas hard clay soil snapped him back around. "I had just hoped that Jake would be more enthusiastic about the boat and some of your toys."

"The kid's a little young to set loose on the Wave Runner."

"You didn't really just say that?" Eve felt her brows inch up her forehead. "How old were you when you beat Mitch for the family championship?"

One side of her brother's mouth curled upward in a knowing smile. "Hey, not every kid is a natural born athlete like yours truly."

"Oh brother. Talk about an inflated ego."

"I beg your pardon?" His hand on his heart, Kyle had the audacity to look offended before laughing and shaking his head.

Addison, Kyle's wife, rolled her eyes at her husband, and shaking her head, kissed him on the cheek. "Such a ham. Good thing I love you." Patting his hand gently, she turned to face Eve. "I will say one thing, if anyone on this ship can relate to kids, it's Craig."

Kyle nodded. "The man does basically play for a living."

"Pot calling kettle black?" She smiled at her brother.

Kyle rolled his eyes. "By now I'm sure Craig's engaging Jake in a favorite video game or some such thing to help the kid take his mind off his grandmother."

When they picked Jake up from camp, Jared had done a remarkable job of explaining to the little boy that his grandmother wouldn't be home for at least a short while. For the most part, Jake listened carefully and only dared ask a few basic questions about hospitals and Mary's injuries, but by the time they were climbing into the car for the ride home, Jake's silence either meant he was at peace with the situation or completely distraught, and she didn't have a clue which it might be.

Unfortunately for everyone, once they parked at the marina, Jake had appeared less than impressed with the big boat, showed little interest in the Wave Runners parked aboard, or the suggestion of tubing on the small motorboat. Fishing hadn't captured his interest either. Eve had thought every little boy was genetically inclined to want to speed, get dirty, and put worms on a hook. Apparently, all of her expectations were dashed at the perpetual blank expression on Jake's face. Though she did think that she had caught a glimpse of interest in his eyes as they'd walked past the bridge, but then Craig had appeared talking about his latest challenge getting permits to light a beach scene in a recent production and the little boy slipped back into his previous state of disinterest.

Shortly after that, Craig offered Jared and Jake a tour of the yacht and since she already knew as much about the boat as her brother, she opted to stay in the lounge with Kyle, thinking the fewer people along for the tour, the more likely the possibility that Jake and Jared might find something to bond over. Something to make the next few weeks more comfortable for both of them.

"Hey man." Kyle pushed to his feet as Jared entered the room. "Long time, no see."

The two men fell into one of those back slapping man hugs that reminded Eve how close the two had once been before Jared took over the Golden Creek. For years they'd partied hard and traded top spots on the most eligible bachelor lists. A good reason why she really shouldn't get so involved, and yet... She studied the two mens' smiling faces. Both men seemed to have manned up and settled down. At least she hoped so.

"I think I may need more help than I thought." Jared turned to the sofa where she sat.

Eve didn't like the sound of that. As inconspicuously as she could manage, she tried to glance around Jared in search of Jake. "What happened?"

"Nothing." He slid into the chair beside her. "He's

talking to the captain about the engines."

"He's talking engines?" She wasn't sure which surprised her more, that Jake was interested in the ship's engines, or that he was talking at all.

Glass paused at his lips, Kyle raised a single eyebrow in her direction.

"Why would the captain be boring a little kid talking about the engines?"

"Bored isn't the first word to come to mind." Jared leaned back in his seat. "Probably because Jake asked him something about nautical miles and the next thing I knew, the two of them were talking as if they were old navy buddies. The kid really seems to know quite a bit about engines, or he's very good at faking it."

"Really?" That had not been what Eve was expecting. Especially not from a nine-year-old. "I'm going to go with he does like boats." If nothing else, the alternative that he was faking an understanding of the ship's engines left her with images of a future con man feeling out his mark, and that was just crazy.

"I think," Jared blew out a short sigh, "he likes anything mechanical."

"And why will you need our help?"

Jared's gaze lifted to Kyle's. He'd almost forgotten he'd mentioned needing help when he'd joined them in the lounge. At least Eve's brother had enough manners not to point out that his previous comment was most likely directed at just her not her and Kyle. "You want to know anything about ranching, I'm your go-to guy." He paused and smiled. "And maybe if you want to know about cars, but engineering, not so much."

"Did you say cars?" Interest sparked in Kyle's eyes.

"He owns a Porsche GT-3 RS."

Lips tight in an approving smile, Kyle nodded. "Nice set of wheels."

"I think so." Jared smiled back.

"In college, all you ever drove was the ranch pickup."

Jared hefted a lazy shoulder. "I went shopping for practical, came home with heaven on asphalt."

"Wait a minute, y'all." Eve waved her hand between the two. "Circle back to what's important. Why aren't you with Jake and what happened to Craig?"

"Craig had to take an important call and the captain's cabin is smaller than you'd think. I was basically told there was no room for me, and that Craig would bring Jake up here when he was finished with his tour."

"There's room for Craig but not you?" That made no sense to her.

"No. Craig's leaning over the landing yelling at someone about a budget and postponing his flight back to the set. I considered waiting outside the cabin door for him, but didn't want to intrude on his conversation."

"Nonsense. Craig should have taken the call elsewhere."

"Maybe. He mumbled something about reception on the yacht before turning his back to us."

That much she knew was true. Her cell phone rarely worked from most places inside the ship.

The intercom phone buzzed and Kyle picked up. "Yes… Uh huh… Thanks."

Nothing like eavesdropping on a man of few words.

"That was the captain. He said that Craig took the boy to the game room. Suggested we join them up deck."

Craig really was the most adept at dealing with kids. The lounge was perfectly peaceful and comfortable for adults, but didn't hold a great deal of promise for a young boy. She pushed to her feet, reached for her cola, and smiled at the two men. "Shall we go?"

"No point avoiding the firing squad." Jared smiled to soften his words. She knew he was teasing, and yet, there seemed to be a hint of sincerity in his words. He finished the last of his tea in one long gulp and stood.

"I don't think it's going to be that bad." Kyle slapped his once upon a time party wing man on the shoulder. "Y'all will find your footing and before you know it, Mary will be home and everything will be well."

Oh, how he hoped Eve's brother was right. After all, what the heck did he know about parenting kids?

CHAPTER ELEVEN

Despite the sense of calm and tranquility that usually came with a day on any of the family boats, even before they'd picked Jake up at camp, today had felt like walking on egg shells. Every step was carefully thought out and executed. She knew Jared felt the same way by the strength with which he'd gripped her hand as they maneuvered their way to the yacht's game room.

Walking at her side, his grip strong but not so steady, Jared leaned in, his voice low, "Thank you."

"Any time." She squeezed his hand and then smiled up at him. "What did I do?"

For the first time all day he chuckled and flashed a real smile. Not the put-on smile to reassure Jake, but a deep from the heart smile that creased the corners of his eyes and made the dark blue irises sparkle with amusement. "Just being you. Being here."

"Can't think of any place I'd rather be."

Now he squeezed her hand again and pulled her just a shade closer to him. Taking a moment to look over his shoulder at her brother Kyle on their heels, Jared blew out a slow, heavy sigh. Whether it was from his concern for young Jake or if he'd felt the need to kiss her as strongly as she wanted to kiss and reassure him, she had no idea.

"What took you so long?" Craig sat across from Jake, cards in his hands, a pensive crease between his brows.

"It didn't take us that long." Kyle crossed the room and pulled the drapes open wider to let in more light.

"What is everyone doing up here?" Addison, Kyle's wife, bounced into the room, a bright smile on her face. She immediately honed in on her spouse and with an affectionate but discreet hug, gave him a quick peck on the cheek, but not before Eve's brother drank his wife in with his eyes. The sheer adoration made Eve want to swoon with envy.

As if he could read her mind, Jared gave her hand another squeeze. The warmth that rushed through her had her lips tipping upward in a contented smile and her cheeks flushing with heat.

"Playing cards." Craig didn't take his eyes off the cards in his hand.

"I love cards." Addison pulled away from her husband and slid into an empty chair and smiled at Jake. "Who do we have here?"

Focusing on his cards, the kid remained silent.

"This is Jake, my housekeeper Mary's grandson." Jared flashed a less than easy smile.

"Nice to meet you, Jake." Addison waited a beat for the boy to say something and then turned to Craig. "What are we playing? Rummy."

Craig shook his head. "Poker."

"Poker?" Eve and Jared both said. Her voice came out a little stronger than she'd intended. Her sentiments echoed in the same stressed tone in Jared's voice.

"I'll see you and raise you two." Craig didn't bother to look up at anyone but Jake, he was so focused on his hand that anyone would easily believe they were playing in some championship game.

Jake scribbled something on a notepad at his side and laid his full house down on the table in front of him.

"How the heck do you keep doing that?" Craig laid his three of a kind down on the table. "How much am I in for?"

Jake didn't glance at the paper, but confidently announced, "Two hundred and twelve dollars."

"We didn't leave you guys alone that long." Jared let go of her hand and slowly walked over to the card table. "How did you lose so much so fast?"

"He's not a little boy." Craig gathered up the cards. "He's a card shark in kid's clothing."

Kyle pulled out a chair by his wife. "You're just a lousy

card player. Deal me in.”

“Wait a minute.” Eve waved her hands in front of her before pointing an accusatory finger at her brother. “You taught him to play poker?”

Shuffling the deck, Craig shook his head. “Nope. It was the kid's idea.”

Eve glanced in Jake's direction and noticed him already cutting the cards. *Well.*

“Where did you learn to play poker?” Jared stood over Jake's shoulder.

“My grandmother,” were the first words the little boy had spoken directly to Jared since stepping onto the gangway.

“Mary taught you?” The surprise in Jared's gaze would be obvious to any stranger.

Jake nodded and after everyone anted up, he waited till all five of his cards were in front of him before looking at his hand. For an instant he looked much older than his young years. His grandmother had apparently taught him well.

One by one, first Jared, then she, then Paige joined them shortly after she'd come aboard. Fascinated, Eve watched as Jake won hand after hand. With every bet or fold, it was as if he knew exactly what cards the other players held. At one point she actually looked around the room to see if there were any mirrors that could be helping Jake out. Nothing.

“Too rich for my blood.” Paige pushed away from the table. “I think I'll wait till y'all switch to Gin Rummy.” Her half sister chuckled and came to her feet.

Jared turned his wrist and checked his watch. “We probably should be heading back to the ranch soon.”

“That's a good idea,” Eve agreed.

“Does the kid have school or camp of some kind tomorrow?” Craig glanced up from his cards.

Jared shook his head.

“Y'all should stay on the ship tonight. Then maybe I'll win some of my money back.”

From what she could see of the notepad Jake had at his side, Craig was into the kid for over a grand. Amazing.

"Can we?" For the first time all afternoon, Jake tore his attention away from the game and with deep soulful eyes, focused on Jared. That one look and she knew it was a good thing Jared was in charge because she would probably give those doe-eyes anything they asked for.

"Maybe another time. I didn't bring any change of clothes."

"No worries." Kyle refilled Jake's lemonade. "We've got plenty of spare clothes for just an occasion like this. You'd be amazed how many unexpected guests drop in when you own a boat or a beach house."

The kid's head whipped around from Kyle back to Jared and the first grin she'd seen beamed in Jared's direction. "Can we?"

Jared glanced in Eve's direction. If he was waiting for her opinion, he was going to have a long wait. She considered it the grace of God that despite dysfunctional parents, she and her siblings were more or less normal. With the example her parents had set, she didn't want to make the kind of mistakes that would render her responsible for Jake's therapy bills when he grew up. She hefted one shoulder in a casual I-don't-know shrug, and Jake nodded at her. "I guess so."

She couldn't speak for Jared, but the huge smiled that widened taking over the little boy's face definitely made Eve want to smile too.

By now, Mitch had joined the clan along with their cousin Devlin.

"Is everyone staying the night?" Jared leaned in so no one else could hear.

Taking a moment to glance at her watch, she nodded. "My vote is at this hour, most likely yes."

"What have we got here?" Mitch kissed his sister Paige on the cheek, then came around the table to do like wise with Eve. When he focused on the cards in Jake's hands, he turned back toward Eve and frowned.

She shrugged. "Craig's the biggest loser so far."

"I beg your pardon." Craig briefly leveled his gaze with his brother. "The kid's luck has to change eventually."

Carefully watching the boy, Eve wasn't all that sure luck had anything to do with it.

In just a few hours, Jared had learned more from watching Jake than he could ever have learned from Mary. On the few occasions the woman spoke of her grandson, he was described as a sweet little boy, quiet, and even though he seemed to struggle at school, she was terribly proud of him. Jared couldn't quite put his finger on what it was, but something was not adding up.

"If you'll excuse me a moment, I need to call the house and let Cook know we're not coming home. She was going to bake a cake for Jake."

Eve nodded at him. From the way she kept her gaze on Jake, Jared suspected that Eve had many of the same questions he did.

His conversation with Cook had been short and to the point. The spare room across the hall from Jared was ready for Jake. Cook and her husband, who lived in another cottage on Gold land, had moved some of the things from Jake's room to the family house so he'd feel more at home. He should have thought of it himself, but was thankful so many people had his back.

"So what's the plan now?" While he was on the phone on deck with Cook, Eve and a few of the adults had moved outside. Jared slid into a deck chair beside Eve.

"We're going to have dinner served up here."

"Yes," Paige nodded at Jared, "Craig managed to learn that pizza is Jake's favorite food."

"So we're ordering pizza?" Jared asked.

Eve shook her head. "Kitchen has a pizza oven."

"That'll work." He had to ask himself if all yachts came with pizza ovens. For some crazy reason he always thought a ship's galley would be small and compact compared to the opulent trappings of a vessel of this size. Now he knew for sure, no kitchen with a pizza oven was going to be matchbox size.

"That's some kid." Devlin came out onto the deck, his cousin Mitch on his heels.

Jared looked over his shoulder, expecting to see Craig and Jake in tow.

"They've moved on to chess." Mitch took a seat at the patio table.

"Chess?"

Devlin nodded. "Craig finally had to take a bathroom break and wouldn't let the game continue without him."

"I thought he was just playing with the salt shakers." Addison sat at the table with Mitch. "I figured it was just a quiet kid entertaining himself."

"I don't think I'm following." Eve glanced over at Jared before looking back at her sister-in-law.

"Apparently," Addison pulled a chair closer to set her feet on, "he was using the salt and pepper shakers as chess pieces."

"How'd you figure that out?" No matter how Jared tossed that information around in his head, he couldn't picture making the connection between playing with condiments equating with chess. Though it could be mostly because he'd never mastered the strategy behind a chess game.

"I didn't." Addison waved her thumb over her shoulder.

"I did." Mitch took a slow sip of a longneck beer.

Eve's brow buckled. "*You* did?"

"Don't look so surprised. I may keep busy but I still remember how to play. Though I admit it took a few minutes to connect the dots, but after watching him for a short while I realized there was a pattern and then it struck me." Mitch shrugged. "So I pulled a chess set out from the cabinet and now the kid and Craig are playing chess."

"You mean Craig gave up on winning his money back?" Paige chuckled softly.

"I didn't say that. I think I heard something about double or nothing as I left them at the chess board."

"Did you by any chance know that he plays chess?" Eve leaned forward, her question directed at Jared.

Jared shook his head. "Admittedly, I don't know a

whole heck of a lot of anything right about now, but this might explain a few things."

"Like?"

"Mary mentioned more than once that he struggled with school. I assumed he wasn't very bright and was challenged with his classes. When I spoke to Cook just now, she mentioned finding time to take him shopping for new school clothes. Apparently, she was hoping shopping without his grandmother might help him fit in better, make friends. She clarified for me that his grades are quite high."

"So," Eve leaned back again, "what he struggles with isn't classes but fitting in. He's actually a really smart kid."

"That shouldn't come as much of a surprise." Mitch tipped his head and shoulder. "My money's on the reason he's winning is because his mind is a bit like a computer. He can count cards. I'm pretty sure, if the kid isn't a genius, he's dang close."

Up until now, with less than a day together, Jared had felt out of his league. Now he knew beyond any doubt that he was in way over his head. All he'd hoped for before today was that Mary would wake up and everything would return to normal. Right about now, he'd pay big bucks for Mary to sit up and tell him what to do. He couldn't help but wonder if she even knew just how smart her grandson was. He had no idea what to make of all this newly found information, and really wished Mary would open her eyes and tell him how to do right by her grandson.

CHAPTER TWELVE

Under normal circumstances, Eve loved sleeping on the *Baroness*. Even though you couldn't really feel the boat rocking, she always felt as if her subconscious knew the ship was lulling her to sleep. Yet, never had she tossed and turned as much as she had last night. This morning she was more tired than she'd been when she'd gone to bed.

A rap on her cabin door reminded her she was late for breakfast. "Coming."

Flinging the door open, Jared stood in the hall. "Jake is gobbling down breakfast. Apparently French toast is his favorite."

"Great. Sorry I'm running late. Just couldn't get a sound sleep."

"You're not late. The others are trickling into the dining room. Like any typical kid, Jake is an early riser and a bottomless pit."

She slipped into one shoe, then hopped sliding the other shoe on. "I'd better get moving. What's Jake doing now?"

"He and Mitch are playing chess. Paige is practically pinning Craig down in the dining room to keep him from playing more cards. I don't know who's the bigger kid, Craig or Jake."

"He wants to win his money back?" The competitive streak in the Baron DNA was deep and strong.

"I think it's more the principle of win and lose than the actual money. Especially when he's getting the pants beat off him by a nine-year-old."

She nodded. That was probably true. Craig could afford to lose a lot more than a thousand dollars. Besides, she was pretty sure Jared wasn't going to let the kid take Craig's money anyhow. Standing upright, she blew out a breath and smiled. "I'm ready. What's the plan?"

"I thought it best if we head out this morning. I'd like to get Jake settled in and prevent him winning anything else from Craig."

"Okay." Her heart did a little dip. She'd hoped that by spending the night on the ship, they'd get to spend more time together today. Earlier she'd sent a text to Isabel letting her know she wouldn't be in.

"I, uh," he inched into the room, "was hoping you'd come back with us. You know, help me smooth over the edges with Jake."

While she loved that he wanted her to go with them, she had no idea what good she'd be with Jake. "Of course I'll do whatever you need, but not sure that I know anything more than you do about dealing with nine year old boys. Probably even less since I've never been a little boy."

The last line made Jared chuckle. "No." He laughed a little harder. "You most definitely were not a little boy, but if Mitch is right about his ability to track and predict cards, he's crazy smart."

"So it seems."

"And even though I'm no slouch, science and math were never my forte. On the other hand, you must have a degree in, what, Chemistry? Physics? Calculus?"

There was no point in mentioning she actually had a PhD in both chemical engineering and computer science. "Something like that."

"Thought so. Will you join us?"

Truth was that she had no idea if her tagging along was the best plan of action, but heading back to the ranch made as much sense as anything else. "As soon as I get a cup of coffee and some protein, we're out of here."

Stepping the rest of the way into the room, he let his hands skim down the side of her arms until their fingers linked together. Squeezing her hands, he leaned in for a slow and tender peck on the lips before easing back. "Thank you."

"There you are." Fork in hand, Paige smiled up at her sister. "I wondered if you were going to sleep the day away."

"It's only nine o'clock in the morning." She slid into a seat beside Craig who was working on a fresh batch of French toast. "Just grabbing a quick bite and then we're heading back to the ranch."

His fork halfway to his mouth, Craig paused to glance in Jared's direction. Jared nodded and her brother returned a little less enthusiastically to his food.

Another short while, lots of hugs and suggesting another day in the future on the *Baroness* would be fun, even if it cost Craig a small fortune, and they were on their way back to the peace and quiet of ranch country.

For the entire ride back to the house, Jake sat quietly in the back seat playing with his tablet. Every so often Eve would twist to check on him. Somewhere in the back of her mind, remnants from some of her psych classes screamed at her that too much screen time was never good for young kids. It took her a lot to limit the way she used her cell so as not to overdo screen time for herself. Of course, the house rules at the ranch of keeping phones tucked away didn't hurt any. She'd have to remember to talk to Jared about it. It wouldn't surprise her to learn that the poor kid's lack of social skills were directly related to the amount of time he spent exercising his brain instead of his body.

As the vehicle drove under the iron arches of the Golden Creek ranch, she glanced in the rear seat once again, in time to catch Jake eyeing the house and for a brief flash, almost smiling. "When will I get to see MeeMaw?"

Wasn't that the million-dollar question.

"She's still sleeping so her body can heal." Jared met the boy's gaze in the rear view mirror. "As soon as we get you settled into the house, I'll check with the doctors and see if there's any update on when we can visit."

The kid nodded and without a smile or flinch or single sign of what he might be thinking, returned to his tablet.

"Home sweet home." Jared put on a wide smile, but Eve had come to know him well enough to recognize the forced effort. "I'll get the bag out of the back."

She met Jared by the hatch as Jake stepped out of the car, never looking up from the tablet. "Do you think he's always this quiet?"

Taking in a long deep breath and blowing it out slowly, Jared shook his head. "I haven't a bloody clue. Wish I did."

She knew exactly how he felt. Eve was very good at what she did. The Barons were used to excelling at their chosen fields and even at their hobbies, but not until now did she realize just how darn little she knew about children.

The front door swung open and Cook appeared in the doorway. A bright smile on her face, and arms open wide, she ran down the front steps and folded Jake in her bosom as if he were her grandson, not Mary's. "Welcome home. I made your favorite peanut butter cream cookies."

Squeezing the woman's middle harder than he might have normally, Jake pinched his eyes shut and seemed to be drinking in the comfort this smiling woman had to offer.

When he finally let go, Cook stepped back. "Only two weeks at camp, and my how you've grown."

Eve had to bite back a grin when Jake rolled his eyes. Something told her this was familiar repartee for the little boy.

"Did you have lots of fun?" Cook swung an arm around the boy's shoulders and nudged him toward the house. "I bet the campfires were great under all those stars."

Jake gave a non-committal shrug.

"And the S'mores? I bet they weren't as good as mine."

This time Jake did smile and still snuggled against her side, shook his head.

The older lady was still talking to the boy when they crossed the threshold and disappeared into the kitchen. Maybe things were looking up for Jake already. At least, she sure hoped so.

After placing Jake's bag in his new room, Jared took a

minute to look around. Cook had done a great job of making the ordinary guest space look like a little boy's room. Still, a few things struck him as odd. Mostly, the lack of traditional toys. At nine years old, Jared's room had scattered sports equipment with the occasional Transformer or Power Ranger. Jake's temporary bedroom had 1,000-piece puzzles, books—not children's books—real books that Jared didn't touch till high school or even college. On top of that, there were some impressive models. If he were a betting man, he'd be wagering on Jake being the poster boy for Future Engineers of America.

"What you thinking?" Eve came up beside him and rested her hand on his forearm.

"I'm more convinced than ever that this kid is more up your alley than mine."

Her brows crinkled together. "How so?"

He took a moment to wave his arm across the wooden and Lego models. "We suspected math, and now I'm adding science to the kid's skill set."

To his surprise, Eve didn't immediately counter his statement. Instead, she took in the items that he presumed had come from Mary's apartment, slowly nodding. "Yep. One special kid. And despite what you suspect, I think we're both out of this kid's league."

Back in the kitchen, Jake was happily eating cookies and playing—at least Jared assumed he was playing—on the tablet. For all Jared knew, his new ward might very well be calculating a cure for cancer or designing a rocket for Mars. All the times he'd walked past Jake in this exact same situation and he'd never taken the time to notice exactly what the kid was doing. "I have to check on the horses. Want to tag along?" He had no idea why he'd asked, but he couldn't help but think, even though he just got back from camp, the kid needed to get out more. The best parts of Jared's childhood involved dirt, mud, creeks, and horses.

Jake's head snapped up, his mouth dropped slightly open, and his head bobbed up and down.

The honest curiosity made Jared smile. "When you finish your cookies, come on out to the barn."

The short bob of the boy's head was no surprise, but seeing him shove an entire homemade cookie into his mouth and spring out of his seat had shocked the dickens out of Jared.

Eve's soft chuckle drifted over his shoulder. "I think you've got this covered. If you don't mind, I'll make myself at home in the living room with my laptop and try to catch up a bit on work."

That made sense. As much as he liked the idea of having Eve around a whole lot, he couldn't just presume she'd always be there when he needed her. "Thanks."

Her smile brightened. "No problem."

"So…" Jared held the back door for the kid and hoped that he'd made the right choice asking Jake to join him. A little too late, his mind started playing through all the reasons why a barn housing full-sized horses could be a dangerous place for a child with no experience with horses. "You like horses?"

The question was clearly more of a challenge for him than math or science because he took a minute longer than he should have to nod.

"Good." Jared stopped and grabbed a couple of apple biscuits from a container and handed them to Jake. "Put these in your pockets."

At first, Jake quietly watched as Jared chatted a few minutes with his foreman before bringing Sugar out of her stall and putting her in the cross ties for a good brushing.

He'd grabbed two buckets and set one down in front of Jake, talking him through the steps of caring for the beautiful animal's coat and hooves, pausing here and there to coo comforting words to the mare.

Jake's gaze focused intently on the horse as Jared spoke. "Do you think she understands you?"

Jared smiled. "Absolutely, and don't let anyone tell you otherwise."

With a nod, the little boy seemed to consider the words and continued to follow Jared's caring example.

"Remember to stay slightly to her side so she can see you. You don't want to spook the horse and be surprised by a strong and painful kick in some unpleasant places."

"Have you ever been kicked?"

"Oh, yeah." He smiled at the boy and was rewarded with the first bright smile he'd seen on the child's face. "There isn't a rancher on the planet who hasn't learned a few lessons the hard way."

Again, Jake nodded and continued carefully helping to brush Sugar down. Done cleaning out the sweet horse's hooves, Jared showed Jake how to give the beautiful animal a treat. "Now it's time to reward her with the treats in your pocket." He waited for Jake to retrieve the carrot-flavored treat. "Make sure to hold your hand flat, then hold it under her nose."

When Sugar's lips tickled his palm, Jake looked up at Jared, a smile on his face and a twinkle in his eyes.

By the time they'd finished with Sugar and moved on to Pepper, Jake and Jared had developed an unexpected rapport. The kid asked question after question. Questions that took Jared by surprise, that he would have expected from another rancher, not from a little boy. But his favorite part were the smiles and giggles. Both his and Jake's. Especially when the little boy in Jake came out at the sight of a kitten. His eyes lit up and he started in the cat's direction, then stopped short.

"Misty, one of our barn cats, had a litter a few weeks ago."

Jake's gaze remained on the kitten, now accompanied by a second sibling.

"If you'd like, they'll play with you."

The boy's head snapped around, and eye's bright with interest now sparkled with excitement.

"Go on." This was the first thing Jared had seen the child do that actually reminded him of a little boy and not a short adult.

The kid took off at full speed and within minutes he was surrounded by playful bouncing kittens while mama cat sprawled comfortably in the doorway sun light. A few more minutes and the kittens were scattered everywhere, climbing up and down the stacked hay bales with Jake chasing after them like a kid playing blind man's bluff. The whole scene made Jared smile. He'd never taken much time to consider a family of his own. Sure, he assumed someday he'd marry and have a family, but someday was an elusive point in time that had little to do with his here and now.

An unexpected swell filled his chest. A joy at watching this bright child enjoy the simplest thing in life made him want to crow with delight like a rooster on a rooftop. He couldn't begin to fathom how he'd feel if this actually were his son and not just a boy temporarily in his care. Suddenly, he understood, even more than before, why the work folks like his mother and Eve did were so important to the circle of life. He'd planned to drive out to West Texas in a few weeks to check out some horses. Maybe he'd move that up. Take Jake on a little road trip. How many boys and girls were there in this world whose lives could be turned around with a short week spent on a ranch with horses and kittens. Maybe he should get a few goats too. Or chickens.

He shook his head. Or maybe he should stick to what he knew—horses, cattle, and barn cats.

"You look awfully pensive." Like an angel summoned from heaven just for thinking of her, Eve appeared in the sunlit doorway.

"Hey there." He didn't bother with the normal pleasantries and politely restrained chivalry. At this moment, in a backdrop of golden sun, she was irresistible. Taking two long strides in her direction, he swooped her into his arms and kissed her with all the emotion coursing through his veins. Like a rod attracting lightening in a storm, it struck him that his someday had just collided with his here and now.

"Stanley, no," a small voice cried in the distance.

Reluctantly, he pulled back from Eve and in a kiss-addled fog, wondered who Stanley was.

Loosely held in his arms, Eve stiffened and her eyes widened, not in delight but fear.

Spinning about, he heard Eve scream Jake's name at the exact same moment his gaze landed on the little boy chasing a kitten up to the loft. Like watching a slow-motion movie, his heart nearly stopped as Jake lost his footing and arms flailing, flew back ever so slowly through the air. No matter how fast Jared's legs ran, there was no stopping the smacking sound of soft child landing on hard floor, or the shrill that escaped Eve's lungs. Dear Lord, not again.

CHAPTER THIRTEEN

Doors slammed, footsteps fell, and pretty much anyone within shouting distance was running into the barn. Eve hurried to Jake's side, only a step behind Jared.

"What happened?" Cook called out, coming to a screeching halt at their side, her eyes rounding and her hands flying to cover her open mouth.

Already, Jared was whipping off his shirt and applying pressure to the long gash on Jake's temple gushing deep red blood.

Eve reminded herself that head wounds bleed—a lot. She tried telling herself it was okay, that Jake would open his eyes any moment and all would be well, but she could taste the panic rising to the back of her mouth. "I'll call 911."

"No time." Jared looked up to Cook, her hands clasped as her lips muttered a soft but constant prayer.

Randy the foreman hadn't made it fully into the barn when he turned and shouted over his shoulder to Jared, "I'll get the truck."

"If we're going to transport him ourselves," Eve reached down and held the child's hand, "we should stabilize him on a board, in case…" She sucked in a slow breath and fought back the threat of tears. "In case he's got more severe injuries."

Jared nodded. "There are some spare boards in the tack room."

"I'll get one." Cook ran across the barn and flung open a closed door.

At the same time, she reappeared with a suitable board

covered in a horse blanket, the foreman eased the truck into the barn and jumped out. "I figure one of us should ride in the back with him."

"I will." Eve pushed to her feet while Jared and Randy carefully shifted Jake onto the board and then into the bed of the truck.

"Here's another blanket." Cook handed it to Eve. "Cocoon him in it. Hopefully that will keep him from moving about."

"Thanks." Eve accepted the blanket and placed it over the terribly pale and still unconscious child.

"We'd better both ride in back. It's going to be a bumpy ride." Jared turned to his foreman. "You'd better drive. And take it easy till we get to the main road."

Jared's shirt was soaked through with Jake's blood, but the gusher appeared to be slowing to a stop. If only the kid would wake up.

Despite the adrenaline rush still coursing through her veins, her mind did a tug of war, jumping from the multitude of sensations enveloping her from one short toe-curling kiss to the slow-motion replay of the little boy falling from the loft. The long drive to the nearest hospital gave Eve too much time to consider all the negative possibilities. Anything from spinal cord damage to brain injuries ran through her mind.

"He'll be okay." Carefully, Jared covered her hand with his and squeezed. Offering words of reassurance as if he'd just read her mind.

Taking the turn into the hospital parking lot a tad faster than he should have, Randy pulled up to the ER and sprang out of the front seat. "I'll get help."

Jared nodded and Eve noted the older man had to be as frightened as she was. A slow meander was the typical speed for the average Texas native. For this situation, Randy ran inside the building faster than a major league ball player rounding third and heading home.

Even though the bleeding appeared to have stopped, Jared didn't dare stop applying pressure to the wound. Eve went ahead and climbed out the back of the pick up and lowered the tailgate just as the staff from inside hurried up to the truck pushing a gurney. Randy on their heels, hopped back into the driver's seat. She'd feel so much better if Jake would wake up.

She and Jared followed after the team. Randy called out to them, "I'll park and circle back."

"The front desk is going to need information from you."

Her eyes glued to Jake's still form, she didn't notice who spoke, but assumed it was the same person waving an arm at two women sitting by computers on the other side of a long counter.

Another nurse rushing alongside glanced at Eve. "You'd better wait here."

And that was it. Jared slowed his steps, his gaze darting from the registration desk on the left to the gurney disappearing down the hall ahead of him.

"I'm sure they'll tell us as soon as they know something." It was a lame thing to say, but she'd hoped that an update was coming sooner than later. What she really wanted was for the little boy to jump up and come running out the door shouting April fools. Fat chance of that in the middle of August. All she could think of now was, what would they tell Mary if anything happened to that little card shark?

Fingers clacking away on the keyboard, without looking away from her screen, the woman behind the desk casually muttered, "I'll be with you in a second."

Jared nodded. He may have grunted as well, but he felt trapped in a numbing cloud. Why hadn't he been paying closer attention?

"There we go." The woman smiled and turned to face Jared. "I need some basic info. What's your son's name?"

"Jake Harlow. And he's not my son."

The woman's gaze narrowed and turned to Eve. "Are you his mother?"

Her hand curling gently around his, Eve shook her head.

The lady's frown deepened as she returned her attention to him. "Are you his guardian?"

"Not exactly."

The frown finally slipped and her brows arched high on her forehead. "Define 'not exactly'."

"His grandmother is his guardian."

"I see. And where's the grandmother?"

"Fifth floor."

"Oh, she works here." A relieved smile took over the woman's face.

"No. She's a patient in ICU."

The frown returned. "All right. Let me get more information."

For the next few minutes, Jared gave the woman what little information he had. He knew the boy was covered under Mary's insurance because he paid for the policy, but all he could tell the woman was the carrier's name. He also had no clue what Jake's social security number was, the exact date of his birth, or if he had allergies to any medication. Other than knowing his full name and address, there was little Jared could offer.

"I'll be right back." She pushed away from her workstation and hurried through a set of double doors.

"Houston, I think we've got a problem." He kept his gaze on the doors the woman had walked through, and kept his grip tight on Eve's hand.

"Let's not go borrowing trouble just yet, but I'll call the Governor. You know, just in case."

Jared nodded. He had a strong feeling that this might be one of those times when who you know helped, and the Governor was a very big who.

"That won't be necessary," the deep voice of Eve's grandfather rumbled behind him.

The Governor had not only entered the building as if he was a brigadier general organizing his troops, his troops were following him in the door.

"I called the Governor before we left the house. Thought he might want to know what was happening."

Bless Cook, the woman was slight in stature but like Mary, big in heart and always had his back.

"Are you all right, dear?" Lila Baron sidled up to her granddaughter.

"It's not me I'm worried about." Eve didn't let go of his hand, but her gaze drifted to the direction the gurney had disappeared down.

"Children are resilient."

He didn't dare say the first thing that came to mind, *but not immortal.*

"We'd better have a seat. I'll see if I can find out what's going on." The Governor waved a hand in the general direction of the waiting room while his gaze scanned the area. Shaking his head, he opted instead to pull out his phone.

Jared had no idea who the man was calling as he walked out of eavesdropping distance. All he could see was the man scowling and nodding.

Another minute or so and the woman behind the desk returned to her position, a nurse following on her heels. "Mr. Gold?"

Jumping to his feet, Jared hurried up to her. "That's me."

The Governor inched closer, his ear still attached to his cell phone, but his attention clearly focused on what the nurse was about to say.

"The boy is conscious."

He could hear every person in the waiting room blow out a relieved breath. Much of the tension that had settled between his shoulders and spiraled up his neck slid away.

"We're going to run some tests to make sure there are no internal injuries, no brain bleeds…"

His mind fixated on brain bleeds.

"The problem," she continued, "is that you are not his guardian. We're of course treating him under emergency conditions, but if we can't get authorization from the person legally responsible for him, we're going to have to call in social services before he can be released."

Even though he nodded calmly, he knew exactly what

she was implying, and also knew that unless Mary woke up unexpectedly, that authorization was going to be slow coming.

The Governor narrowed his gaze, and as the woman once again disappeared behind the double doors, he turned back up the hall to continue his conversation.

"Now what?" Eve whispered.

"I have no idea." But one thing he was sure of, doing nothing wasn't an option. An advantage of being one of the larger ranches in this part of the state, and having a father who played corporate games better than he raised cattle, was that the family had a plethora of good lawyers. Now, he simply needed to find the right one.

His phone in his hand, he scrolled through his contacts, when the Governor set his hand on Jared's arm. "I've got the ball rolling on this."

Of course, Jared didn't have a clue what ball the Governor was rolling, but he did know that the man had more contacts than the almighty himself. For now, he'd sit tight and see how things unfolded, but for Jake's sake, he hoped reality wasn't as dismal as his frenzied imagination.

CHAPTER FOURTEEN

Not sure what else she could do, Eve's thoughts ran to Jake all alone and she leaned over the desk. "Can we go see him now?"

The woman looked horribly confused, or perhaps torn.

The Governor stepped up beside his granddaughter. "The child is most likely very confused by all the strangers."

"Yes, I understand, but only immediate relatives are allowed inside."

"We're as immediate as he has at the moment." Jared stared the woman down.

"I, uh, understand, but," the clerk shook her head, "I don't make the rules."

"Yes." The Governor smiled that knowing grin that Eve recognized all too well. Her grandfather had something up his sleeve. She was positive.

"James." A tall man with salt and pepper hair approached, his arm extended. "So glad I happened to be at my desk."

"Yes. Ed." The Governor smiled at the man. "As discussed, my granddaughter and neighbor want to be inside with the injured boy."

"Yes. I already checked with the nurse's station. He's been taken for a CAT scan. Let me escort you back to the ER and you can wait for him there."

The young lady behind the desk stared wide eyed at the man as if he were stark naked and speaking Martian, but didn't dare say a contradicting word when the four of them followed her grandfather through the double doors and into a small exam room.

It had been ages since Eve had seen the inside of an ER and the lack of curtained areas and move to all private rooms surprised her.

Inside, the Governor gestured for Lila to sit in the one available chair.

"I'll see about getting you a few more seats." Ed turned on his heel.

"Thank you." The Governor nodded.

Once the man was out of sight, Eve turned to her grandfather. "Who exactly is that?"

"Ed Barker heads the board of directors for the hospital."

She should have known. "So everything is fine now?"

The Governor looked to her, then Jared. "So far."

That she didn't like.

"You have any connections with social services?" Jared's tone was almost teasing.

The Governor's lopsided I-know-something-you-don't grin appeared again. "Working on it."

And this was just one of the reasons that Eve worked so many charities. There were perks to being a Baron in this world, perks that not everyone had access to. It was her job to see to it that life went more smoothly for those who didn't have a former governor for a grandfather.

An orderly appeared with two stackable chairs and a moment later another person appeared with one more. With everyone seated, all they could do now was wait.

In short order, gurney wheels could be heard rolling down the hall. Happy for a reason to stretch her legs, Eve pushed to her feet as Jake was brought into the room. A few more moments for a nurse to hook him up to a small monitor and the kid was settled in.

"How ya feeling?" Jared asked.

"My head hurts."

"I bet. That was quite a tumble."

Jake frowned. "I'm sorry. MeeMaw always tells me to be careful."

"Accidents happen," Jared reassured him. "We're just glad you're all right."

"MeeMaw told me that climbing wasn't safe."

Something in the look in the little boy's eyes didn't sit right with Eve, and from the studious glint in Jared's eye, she'd bet he'd noticed it too.

"You have to be particular about where you choose to climb," Jared offered. "And how. There's a ladder to the hayloft that's much more surefooted than stacks of hay."

"The kitten made it look so easy."

Jared shrugged. "Cats are pretty sure footed. They can climb on just about anything, anywhere, and always land on their feet."

"That's because they have a righting reflex, partly due to more vertebrae than humans. The reflex allows them to turn midair and right themselves. Of course, it's also due to their vestibular apparatus in their inner ear that helps them determine up from down and keep their balance even in midair."

The response made Jared smile. When he turned to face Eve, she knew they were both thinking the same thing. Neither of them needed the results of the CAT scan to know the kid really was going to be okay. Though she wouldn't mind knowing what that disturbed look was in his eyes a moment ago.

"Excuse me." Cook knocked on the doorframe. "That nice man said I could come see for myself that our young man is fit as a fiddle."

Jake's eyes sparkled. Apparently, the little boy was as attached to Cook as he was to his own grandmother.

"My, don't you look good." Cook smothered him in an awkward hug and gingerly kissed the uninjured side of his head. "How many stitches?"

Jake muttered, "Twenty-four."

Cook's jaw dropped wide open. "Oh, dear. This is why your grandmother doesn't like you wandering around the ranch. It's a dangerous place for a little boy."

The words pinged around in Jared's mind. No wonder the boy was always in the kitchen or with his grandmother. It was clear to any idiot that the child was off the charts intelligent, at least for a kid his age, but now his lack of interest in the things that would appeal to an average little boy made more sense. Not only was he book smart, but in her desire to protect the last of her family, his grandmother had reeled in his boyhood curiosity.

"Wow, we do have a crowd." The doctor glanced at all the people scattered about the small space.

"Is there an update?"

A tall, slender brunette not quite old enough to be his mother nodded. "CAT scan shows no brain bleeds, no swelling, no internal damages. What we have here is a good hard head and a mild concussion."

"Why was he out so long?" Jared asked.

The doctor shrugged. "No telling, but keep in mind a concussion is no small matter. Under the circumstances, we'll keep him overnight for observation. If all goes as expected, he can be released tomorrow."

Jared really wished the doctor's words brought more comfort, but the man didn't look any happier about Jake's condition than he was. He was unsettled about a great deal of things happening today. "We'll be happy to get him home."

"Yes, well, about that." The doctor shifted in place. "We've notified social services that the child does not have a legal guardian. Someone should be by before tomorrow morning to make a placement."

"Placement?" That uneasy prickle on the back of his neck was spreading rapidly to every pore.

"Yes, I'm afraid he'll have to be placed in a foster home until his grandmother can take custody again."

"That could be months," Eve blurted out before he could say a word.

"I'm afraid it's out of my hands. Hospital policy." Taking a step in retreat, the doctor offered a shaky smile. "The nurse will be back soon to take him to his room. Y'all can go with him and help him settle in, but you're going to have to leave when visiting hours are over."

Jared nodded, not liking the sound of any of this.

As soon as the woman had pulled the door closed behind her, Lila Baron turned to her husband. "James?"

"Yes, dearest. I'm on it."

Those were the five most welcome words to Jared's ears.

Despite Jared's insistence that everyone go home, they all stayed until not only was Jake settled in his new room, but fed as well. Halfway through dinner, Jared came within inches of having to restrain Cook from going to the kitchen and whipping up what she called a 'decent' meal.

"I mean, really." Cook stood with her hands on her hips. "How is anyone supposed to improve eating that slop?"

Apparently, a concussion was grounds for a bland diet, but there was no explaining that to Cook.

Now he worried what was going to happen tomorrow. Not that worrying accomplished anything, but there was no way he was letting social services put Jake in a foster home for one minute, never mind until Mary was up and on her feet.

A tune from a cell phone Jared couldn't quite put his finger on sounded and everyone's head turned to the Governor, who mumbled something that sounded very much like about time. "Excuse me." The man held up a finger and stepped out of the room.

"I wouldn't worry if I were you." Lila Baron smiled at him. "There's no one better to have in your corner."

He had no idea how she knew that whoever he was talking to had something to do with his current dilemma, but he certainly hoped she was right and the Governor was using his vast range of friends and acquaintances to solve the guardianship issue.

"This may not be the best time to tell you, but since we're all here…" Lila glanced a moment at the closed door with her husband's muffled voice on the other side. "As we discussed over the new charity, we really need to do a fundraiser early on to help offset the growing list of expenses."

Jared nodded. With all his distractions this week, he hadn't given any thought to the fundraisers they'd discussed.

"Well, I've had notice from several people and the first event is going to be next Saturday, which gives us just under two weeks to prepare. I expect we'll have just enough time to complete the outrider shack."

He'd completely forgotten that the Governor had ordered an architect to redesign the shack for public use. He knew that bringing the Barons onboard would mean things would happen more quickly than if he squeezed the effort into his already tight schedule, he just hadn't considered how fast a society matron and a retired Marine Corps officer turned politician could move. Since he'd taken a step back to let the Governor and Ms. Lila get the ball rolling, he hadn't given another thought to the remodeling that had begun the other day.

"And of course," Lila continued, "something to show off besides the kids on horseback. Do you think you'll be up to a road trip to pick up a couple of new horses?"

In the next two weeks he wasn't sure he'd be up to rolling out of bed, never mind go shopping for just the right horses. "I'll check with Connor. See what we can do. I gather you want the new horses here before the fundraiser?"

Lila Baron nodded. "That would be helpful, but not a deal breaker. There'll be a simple carnival, petting zoo, and basic trail rides for the kids—which is why more horses would be good. The adults will be plied with plenty of fresh blueberry lemonade and some of my granddaughter Paige's wine." Lila's smile widened. "Of course, she's donating the libations for the cause, and we all know how much more free people are with their checkbooks after a few glasses of good wine."

The first thing to pop into his head was whether or not just under two weeks was enough time to properly pull something like this off, but then he reminded himself who he was dealing with. If there was a human being who could pull off a project of this magnitude this quickly, it was Lila and James Baron. "Sounds good to me."

"And that settles that." The Governor walked into the room, nudging the door closed behind him.

Oh, how he hoped *that* referred to the problem with guardianship and not some other family issue he wasn't privy to.

A broad grin took over Lila's face. "Judge Clifford."

The Governor nodded, but didn't smile or frown or give any other indication if the outcome of his conversation with Judge Clifford was good or bad. Jared's unease must have shown, because all of a sudden, he felt Eve's fingers weave with his. Turning in her direction, he was surprised to realize she'd inched her way across the room without him noticing, but the sweet smile and squeeze of his hand told him that she had more confidence in what the Governor was about to say than he did.

"We can expect to receive his certification of guardianship before the social services rep can find a parking space."

"Certification?" Cook asked.

Again, the Governor nodded. "Normally emergency certification is done through a hearing that can take weeks to get on the dockets. Something that completely belies the concept of emergency, but I digress. Besides my recommendation," the Governor pointed casually in Jared's direction, "the judge played golf a time or two with your father. He didn't need much convincing that you would be a suitable guardian. With Cook's help, of course."

That last comment made the queen of the Gold kitchen smile from ear to ear. "I guess now we can go home and sleep in peace."

Both Cook and Lila Baron stood at the same moment the shift nurse appeared in the doorway. "Visiting hours are over, folks. The young man needs his rest. Y'all can come back first thing in the morning."

Multiple heads bobbed in agreement. Still holding

Eve's hand, Jared stood from his seat by Jake's bed and not letting go of her, using his other hand, he grabbed hold of Jake's thin fingers. "You get a good night sleep. Tomorrow, we'll spring you from this place. Sound good?"

Jake nodded. "At home, can I have some of Cook's banana bread?"

"I'll bake an extra loaf for you," the still smiling lady promised the little boy, putting a matching grin on his face.

"And how would you feel about helping me out tomorrow?" Jared remained at the boy's bedside a moment longer.

"You mean in the barn?" The boy's lips pressed into a thin line. "I don't think MeeMaw would like that."

Jared nodded, but he didn't like it. What good was growing up on a ranch if you never got to do any of the fun things most children enjoy? Whether Mary liked it or not, it was time for the kid to break loose, and Jared was just the man for the job.

CHAPTER FIFTEEN

Coming to work may not have been Eve's best idea. After they'd left the hospital last night, for the short car ride home they kicked around the options for the next day. Since Jared expected to waste hours with social services over guardianship, he didn't see the point in Eve being frustrated alongside him. So here she sat, pretending to work while waiting for Jared to call.

"You're doing it again." Isabel stood in the doorway.

Immediately, Eve focused on the work in front of her. "Doing what?"

"Sitting here but thinking somewhere else."

There was no point in continuing the pretence. She tossed her pen on the table top and rolled away from her work station. "I shouldn't have come in today, should have gone straight to the hospital."

Isabel's eyes rounded as she hurried forward. "What happened? Are you all right? Something broken? Are you in pain? Should I get the car, give you a ride?"

"Whoa." Eve waved her hand at her friend. "Slow down. I didn't mean for me."

"Oh, no. The woman in the hospital? She didn't make it?"

Eve shook her head. "She's still hanging on. This time, my neighbor's ward fell from the hay loft and knocked himself out."

"Uh," Isabel gasped as her hand flew to her heart. "How is he?"

Eve shrugged. "Mild concussion, but the hospital kept him overnight for observation."

"Well, that's good. Kids are surprisingly resilient.

They've been falling out of trees and hay lofts for generations."

"I suppose." She knew deep down that Isabel was right. Heaven knew her own brothers had survived racing boats, riding horses, climbing trees, and a host of other childhood mishaps, including crossing the roof to sneak up on the barn without being noticed by their parents. It was a miracle Kyle didn't kill himself when he fell off and landed on the south side balcony. "I just don't like not knowing what's happening."

"So go."

Eve's gaze shot up to Isabel.

"Why do you look so surprised? You *do* own the place. You're allowed to do whatever you want."

"Maybe."

"No maybe about it. Go." Isabel waved her hand from the Eve to the door. "Just go."

Nodding, she pushed away from the counter and reached into a drawer for her purse. "You're right. I'll check in later."

She'd barely made it two steps when the lab door swung open.

"The nice lady at the front desk said it was okay to come back." With Jake quietly at his side, Jared stood in the same spot Isabel had been in a moment ago. "Is this okay?"

"Absolutely." She dropped her purse on the counter and walked over. Delighted when Jared leaned in for a short but sweet touch of her lips. "I was having a hard time concentrating on work."

"I'm sorry, I should have called. I thought it would be nice to surprise you."

"It's fine. The important thing is Jake was well enough to be released."

Jake didn't move but his eyes tracked the room from one station to another.

"Would you like a closer look?" she asked.

The little boy's head bobbed quickly up and down.

Eve extended her hand to the boy and walked him over to the project she'd been tinkering with. His gaze seemed to intensify as he took in the different tubes and vials along the table top.

"Mr. Gold says you mix perfumes?"

"That's right." Eve smiled, surprised the young child seemed intrigued. Most adults, especially men, had no clue what a complex job it was coming up with new and appealing scents or how easy it could be to create eau of rotten egg.

"My grandmother collects miniature perfume bottles."

"Does she?"

"Mostly Guerlin."

"French perfumes?" Eve didn't know if she should be more surprised that the kid remembered the name of his grandmother's favored perfume or that he'd pronounced it perfectly.

"She has a few other French brands. Givenchy and Chanel, but Guerlin is her favorite. MeeMaw's idea of the perfect vacation is a week stalking the brocantes—flea markets—in France. Though she hasn't gone for a while now."

Eve had to remind herself she was carrying on a conversation with a little kid. Any moment she wondered if he might not break out into a lecture on the history of perfumes, in French. His gaze continued to eye the empty tubes on the counter.

"Do you think maybe for MeeMaw's birthday we could make a perfume just for her? She loves lilacs."

A smile tugged at her cheeks, and lifting her gaze to Jared, Eve noticed he too sported a soft smile even though his eyes reflected a hint of bewilderment. She couldn't blame him, Jake was quite the interesting boy. "I'd be delighted to work with you on a special scent for your MeeMaw."

The kid's face lit up brighter than if she'd offered him a double scoop chocolate ice cream cone with sprinkles. Which made her suddenly wonder if this genius kid even liked ice cream. The next thing she knew they were hovered together over the table top, testing different scents and options.

From behind them, Jared watched over their shoulders. His expression couldn't have shown more pride if the kid had been his.

Content with the care and intensity in which Jake studied each of her vials, Eve dared to step back and speak quietly to Jared. "You know, he seems to have an instinct for this."

"Really?"

"It's not natural for people to know what scents blend together well and he seems to almost intuitively have some pretty good ideas."

Jared shrugged. "I shouldn't be surprised. I'm beginning to wonder if this kid isn't the smartest person I know. Present company excluded."

She shook her head. "Thanks, but he just might be smarter than both of us combined."

Another few minutes and Jake reminded her of a cartoon mad scientist: the way he moved about the lab examining his different options before returning to his seat with new vials and containers. She loved the intent focus as he handled the different ingredients then shaking his head at some, returning them to their rightful place, or bobbing his head at others, pouring the tincture into his efforts.

"I can't believe how much he's enjoying this." Eve chuckled softly. "I may have to hire the kid."

That brought a belly laugh from Jared. "You might also have to get the Governor to intercede on your behalf against child labor laws."

Her next words froze on the tip of her tongue as she spotted the tube of civet in Jake's hand. Diluted civet would add a musky smell, anything more than parts per million and welcome to a multi cat litter box. Then she saw it. Beside him on the table were a row of products that had nothing to do with perfumes and everything to do with cleaning the sinks. Before she could react, he'd poured a goodly amount of multiple items into the tube. Immediately, the serum hissed and like an erupting volcano spewed a cloud of aromas that would make a skunk smell fresh.

"Oh, hell." Jared sprang forward, grabbing the tube and

crossing the room in half the steps it would have taken Eve to reach the sink, dumped the concoction down the drain and turned on the cold water. "Dang, that stinks."

Eve turned to the little boy. "You're not supposed to mix vinegar and baking soda.

Eyes wide and tracking Jared's every movement, Jake lifted his chin to level his gaze with hers. A huge grin stretched across his face. "I know."

Jared didn't know if he should let out the deep-down belly laugh that stirred inside him, or send the kid to bed without supper. The little stinker, literally, knew he was creating a stink bomb. Apparently there was at least some childlike mischief in the kid.

"From now on, no more working in the lab when you're distracted." Isabel came rushing into the room, face mask firmly in place, spraying something in the room, while another tech set out open boxes of some kind of granules.

"Thank you, Izzy." Hand over her mouth, Eve hid a smile.

"Y'all better head on home and wash up. And you'll want to take some of the enzyme with you after you stink up the car."

Eve nudged Jake forward and turned to Jared. "Let's get out of here. They've got this under control."

"What is she spraying?" Jared fell into step beside her.

"It's a special odor absorbing enzyme. It should stop the stench from spreading throughout the ventilation system."

"Really?" He was impressed. Wouldn't mind something like that for the hot days in the barns.

"Well, theoretically. No one has ever set off a stinker like that one before." Sucking on her lower lip, she bit back more of a smile. "I guess we should take one car. No point in smelling up both."

He nodded. "I was going to see if we could coax you into spending the afternoon at Kemah Boardwalk, but I think that will have to wait for another day."

"Agreed." She hit the clicker for her car. "Hop in and I'll drop you off. We can come back for your car later."

"No need. I'll send a couple of ranch hands to get it." He considered his next words. "I have an idea if you're willing."

Her one brow rose high. "That sounds ominous."

"Not so much." He chuckled, shaking his head. "Why don't we drive by your place and grab a swimsuit. I think I have a better way to wash up."

She hesitated just long enough for him to think she might say no, but instead, a grin tipped at the corners of her mouth and she bobbed her head enthusiastically. "No need to stop. I have swimsuits at the ranch."

It didn't take long for them to hand off her car for clean up while they all changed into swimsuits and grabbed towels. Using one of the four wheelers, it wasn't long before the three of them were at his favorite childhood spot on the ranch. "Some years the swimming hole used to run dry, but a few years ago when we redesigned the irrigation system, I made sure there was always water here. At the time, my dad thought it made no sense, but now I'm glad I insisted."

He actually had no idea why it had seemed so important to him. Deep down somewhere his unconscious must have been thinking ahead to when there would be children on the ranch again. That thought brought visions of little kids running across the green wide-open space, swinging from the same tire swing he had, and splashing into the water beside the shady live oak trees. Interestingly enough, those imaginary children had faces that looked like him, or Eve. His mind took that thought and ran with it. Parking under the shade, he was suddenly seeing so many kids running around with Eve chasing after them, laughing at some and reproving others. There was little doubt in his mind that she'd make a great mother. Of course, she'd have to be a wife first.

Any of these thoughts and visions should have sent him running to the hills, but they didn't. As a matter of fact, it warmed him like an aged brandy from head to toe. A wife. *His wife*. Maybe he was losing it. No one shifted to thoughts of marriage with someone they only knew for a couple of weeks. *Right*? He watched her spread the blanket Cook had given them as he carried the basket with a 'decent' lunch. No doubt a feast suitable for royalty. The idea of spending days like this with their own children had grabbed hold of him and simply wouldn't let go. Maybe Jake hadn't been the only one shaken up by his fall.

Their tummies full and the lingering odor of the earlier stink bomb gone, Jared was thrilled to see the young genius give way to the little boy. After a few tepid tries, Jake had finally overcome the fear of getting hurt that his grandmother had so consistently ingrained in him, and taken to swinging from the tree rope into the water like he'd been doing it all his life. He'd mastered catching frogs, digging up worms and fishing for supper. Jared didn't remember ever seeing that kid grin so wide for so long. Jake had gotten dirty, fallen down, gotten up and started the routine all over again multiple times. Now all Jared needed was for Mary to come home and not kill him for taking the fear of God out of her grandson. Actually, he just wanted Mary to come home, period.

Eve reached for his hand, grinned from Jake placing a squirmy worm onto a hook, and over to Jared. "It'll be fine. Mary won't kill you." How she knew what he was thinking baffled him, but he loved her all the more for it. Then her smile widened and she flashed that goofy grin at him. "This time."

CHAPTER SIXTEEN

The next couple of weeks had flown by so fast that Eve didn't have a clue how her grandparents and Jared had pulled this fundraising event off. Somewhere in a busy schedule, Jared had squeezed out a few days to take Jake out to Farraday Stables to pick out a couple of suitable horses for the new program. Every day since their return, Jared had carved out enough time to teach Jake how to care for, saddle, mount and ride a horse. In less than a week the kid was mastering the tasks as well as he'd mastered mixing a stink bomb.

Even now, the scurry of people running about like ants had an order that she would expect from any of her grandfather's military parades.

"I can't believe this is happening." Jared's arm wound around her waist as he leaned into her with a kiss on the temple. "We've received so many donations from people your grandparents and my mom invited who couldn't make it that I almost feel like we don't need to go through with today."

"Glad you added the almost."

He spun her around to pull her fully into the circle of his arms. "This is going to be so much bigger and better than I had imagined."

"The fundraiser or the program?"

"Both."

"Jared." Jake came running up to him. "Can I help tie the ribbons on the calves? Tim says I have to ask you first."

Letting go of her, Jared took a step back and ruffled the top of Jakes head. "Sure."

The little boy glanced in the direction of the house.

"What about MeeMaw?"

Jared's gaze followed the little boy's up to the house and where he and Jared both knew the boy's grandmother was most likely sitting in her wheelchair, watching every move from the guestroom window. "It'll be okay. Go on."

The kid ran off like any other little boy.

"Do you think all the kids who come through here will be transformed like Jake?" Jared kept his arm around Eve's shoulder but his gaze on Jake.

"I sure hope so." Eve leaned into him. "I've always heard horses are excellent therapy animals, but never considered how much we all learned about love and responsibility by growing up with these glorious animals."

Jared bobbed his head. "Ditto."

Hand clapping sounded behind them moments before Lila Baron appeared smiling and sweetly spouting instructions. "Places, everyone. Our guests will begin arriving any minute."

Turning his wrist, Jared glanced at his watch. "Dang, the morning flew by."

Eve's gaze shifted from her own watch to the miscellaneous booths and entertainment set up. "Where are you stationed?"

"Bounce house."

Her cheeks pulled her mouth into a delighted smile. "Imagine that. So am I."

"Mm. Imagine. Didn't Mrs. Baron make up the work schedule?" Jared asked.

Nodding her head in a resounding motion for yes, Eve didn't bother holding back a laugh. "We need to rewrite the old song from Lola to Lila."

"Old song?"

"You know, the one from that baseball movie, 'whatever Lila wants, Lila gets' and my grandmother wants great-grandchildren."

"Right." He shook his head, and holding her hand, made their way over to the bounce house set up close to the patio off the main residence.

"Do you think Mary is still watching out the window?"

Eve unzipped the front flap of the massive contraption.

Jared shook his head and tied back the flap. "Nope. She's probably arguing with the nurse right now that coming down to the festivities isn't too much for her."

"I'm still amazed that after all that time in the hospital, despite the doctor's estimate that she'd need at least a week or two before she moved on to rehab, she was released in what, six days?"

"Five. That woman is a mama bear personified. Come hell or high water, she was coming home to check on her cub for herself."

The families were beginning to amble around the carnival-like set up. All the Barons were helping in some place or other. Paige was at the Corn Hole section, already on her haunches showing a pair of little ones how to toss the square bean bags. That sister of hers probably should have been an elementary school teacher instead of a vintner. She always had the patience of a saint.

"And there you have it." Grinning from ear to ear, Jared gave safety instructions to the two kids who had raced straight for the bounce house, while Eve ensured they'd removed their shoes into the wall of bins set up at the side. Jared lifted his chin toward the house and still smiling, shook his head.

Sure enough, with the day nurse at the helm, Mary came bouncing across the green landscape in her shiny new wheelchair. The woman was certainly feisty. When Eve had heard that Mary refused to go to rehab, she'd been a tad concerned. It was her grandmother who had done the best job of reassuring Eve that Mary would get better attention at home with private physical and occupational therapy than in a huge facility where the nurses were too overworked to give a patient the kind of care the family would want. Fortunately, what Mary's insurance didn't cover, the Golds happily did. From what Eve could see now, the decision had been the right one. The woman had been home less than a week and she already seemed to be holding herself straighter in the seat and waving one arm with more vigor than when she'd left the hospital.

As for what Mary was waving theatrically about, Eve had no idea and wasn't sure she wanted to. Helping another little girl untie her shoes, Eve looked up in time to see Mary's wheelchair pivot left and change trajectory now heading toward the corral with the horse rides—and where Jake's assigned task was to help reassure the younger kids who had never been around horses. "Uh oh."

Jared's head snapped in the direction Eve was staring. He looked from the growing line of kids over to the stables and then his shoulders relaxed and a slight smile reappeared. "Saved by the Baroness."

It took Eve a moment to understand. No one in the family had ever referred to her grandmother as the Baroness. That woman was the family's saving grace and this was no exception. At a quick clip for any woman, never mind one of her years, she was on course to intercept Mary. "Gotta love that woman," Eve whispered.

Jared's gaze shifted to her, his smile brightened, his eyes twinkled, and he winked at her. "The acorn doesn't fall far from the tree."

It took Eve a few seconds to process the implications. Another moment of silence, and kids waiting on line, more kids happily bouncing inside, Jared crossed over the entry to the play house and circled his arms around her waist. For a split second, the intensity of his gaze almost had Eve losing her breath.

"For what it's worth." He tugged her closer to him. "I love you."

Every second seemed to tick by in slow motion. Jared picked one heck of a time, surrounded by crowds of strangers, to tell Eve that he loved her. *No.* It was more than love. He loved his family and friends. He was *in love* with Eve Baron. Debating if he should step back, pretend he hadn't said a word, and get back to tending to the munchkins clamoring to bounce around inside with the other children imagining themselves anything from an astronaut to an acrobat, or pull her in tight and do his best to kiss her till her toes curled.

All set to retreat, he loosened his hold when Eve blinked at him, then easing up on her tippy toes, whispered against his lips, "And I love you."

There was no resisting the temptation. A line of kids as long as the Rio Grande wasn't enough to stop him from tugging her fully against him and pressing his lips ever so gently to hers.

Oblivious to the adult behavior, a little boy tugged on Jared's belt loop. "Is it my turn yet?"

Chuckling softly, Jared let go of the woman he loved and returned to his position on one side of the bounce house entry. "Let's see about this."

No matter how much he tried to focus on the kids coming and going, he couldn't stop looking over at Eve and grinning like the danged Cheshire Cat. She loved him too. Really loved him. He was totally shocked that he was still rooted in place and not floating in air. When Chase and CJ showed up to relieve them, he was truly surprised at how quickly the time had passed. Like a teen on a first date, the opportunity to simply hold her hand on their way to the corrals and the calf chase had made him feel like king of the world.

Before they got to their destination, he dipped left and tugged her into the shadows of the barn. "I'm sorry, but I can't resist." Once again, his arms gently around her waist, he let his lips meet hers. The kiss was soft and sweet and lasted longer than he'd expected, but not as long as he would have liked.

A few more feet and they'd reached the portable bleachers that had been set up for the event. Young children were lined up along the fence line. Bright pink ribbons were tied around the necks of several young calves. The first was released and the little munchkins took off after him. The kids ran circles around the cow, or did the cow run circles around the kids? Jared wasn't sure, but he and Eve were laughing heartily at the group. Finally, one of the cow hands stepped in to help corner the playful calf as one of the taller boys grabbed hold of the ribbon pulling it loose.

The crowd erupted in cheers and another calf and group of children entered the arena and started the song and dance all over again. Not till the third group with young Jake in the mix came out for their turn, and a loud gasp sounded at his side, did Jared realize the nurse had wheeled Mary up beside them.

"Jake is too young." Mary's hand slowly reached out to touch his sleeve. "You have to get my boy out of there."

They hadn't told Mary very much of what was going on. Though she'd grown more aware of her grandson's lack of time in the kitchen, she hadn't quite connected the dots of how much Jake had learned about enjoying life on a ranch.

Carefully squatting down on his heels, Jared let go of Eve's hand and took hold of Mary's. "He's going to be just fine, Mary. He understands being careful even when he's having fun."

Her eyes wide, he tried not to wince at the purse in her lips as she tried to speak. Sometimes the words came easily for her, but the more upset she was, the more likely she was to stammer or freeze.

"Mary. I promise you. It's okay."

By the time Mary's eyes shifted from his to the children running about, Jake had already proved him right. They'd caught a last-minute glimpse of him assuredly trotting after the animal and cutting him off at one side, grabbing a hold of and pulling the pink ribbon until he held it up in the air gripped tightly in his hand as the other kids and calf wandered away.

"See?" The warmth of Eve's hands gently settling on his shoulder made him smile as much as Jake's great performance. "He's going to make a great cowboy. If he wants."

Mary looked from Jared to Eve's hands and frowned ever so slightly as her gaze leveled with his.

Reaching over his shoulder, he squeezed one of her hands and smiled at Mary. "What can I say, I'm irresistible."

With her other hand, Eve smacked his shoulder lightly, then giggled. "Maybe a little."

The interaction brought the first real smile to Mary's face since setting eyes on her grandson after waking up in the hospital. "Good. Very good."

His gaze drew up to meet Eve's then drifted off to the events wrapping up around them. As far as he was concerned, everything was better than good. It was perfect.

EPILOGUE

"Only at the Baron household can a simple birthday feel like a world class event." Siobhan Baron shook her head at her brother.

"Well," Craig smiled, "you gotta admit, we are sort of world class."

His kid sister smacked him on the arm—hard. "Such an ego."

"I beg your pardon?" Craig slapped his hand on his heart and tipped his head back. "You wound me."

"Oh, brother." Siobhan rolled her eyes.

"You rang?" Kyle appeared at Siobhan's opposite side.

"Your brother is being a ham."

Considering Craig was her brother too, Kyle's brow shot up and Craig smiled innocently and shrugged.

Shaking her head, Siobhan muttered 'men' and wandered off toward the far side of the patio set up as a dance floor.

"I don't remember Grams putting this much effort into my thirtieth birthday." Craig kept his gaze on the friends and family meandering about, all smiles and laughter, a handful on their way to three sheets to the wind.

"The girls always get more attention for their thirtieth than the boys. I think to offset a biological clock alarm." Kyle took a sip of his blueberry lemonade.

"Does that still even exist?"

Kyle frowned at his brother. "Does what still exist?"

"Biological clock?" Craig responded.

"You're kidding right?" The look of incredulity on Kyle's face was photo worthy.

"No, I'm not kidding. Women aren't in a hurry to walk

down the aisle anymore and I don't hear anyone warning against starting a family even into their forties."

Kyle shrugged. "Times may be changing, but that biological clock is real. It may kick in later than it used to, but it's still there. I think women just aren't as nervous about hitting the snooze button."

"Snooze button?" A mimosa in hand, Paige came up to her brothers. "Do I want to know what we're sleeping through?"

"Biological clock," the two siblings echoed.

The corners of Paige's mouth tipped up in a cheeky smile in Kyle's direction. "Getting ready to make the Governor a happy great-grandfather, are we?"

Kyle's eyes opened wide and he took a step back shaking his hands. "Oh, no. Don't even think it. Sure, we want kids some day, just not today."

Paige laughed. "Chicken."

"I'm with her." Craig winked at his half-sister.

"Pot calling kettle black?" Kyle turned to his brother. "I don't see you in any hurry to find a wife and start a family."

"Hey, what can I say?" Craig flashed a smug smile. "We're not all willing to drive a woman off the road to find a wife."

"Okay," Kyle sighed, "that was not on purpose."

"Hey, guys." Paige raised both her hands at her siblings. "Let's call a truce."

An older tune from his grandparents' generation played from the speakers the DJ had set up near the dance floor. Craig noticed Eve and Jared stroll onto the floor like a pair of contestants on a TV dance show. "Damn, she looks good."

Paige nodded. "Wait two minutes. Five dollars says they clear the dance floor."

"You're on." Kyle nodded.

Craig frowned. Why the heck would they clear the floor? His gaze fixed on his oldest sister and her beau, he watched their faces. How had he missed how much in love these two were? Their gazes were locked like missiles on heat. As a matter of fact, he wouldn't be at all surprised if the heat in their eyes didn't set everything within a five-foot radius on fire.

"I'd swear, anyone would think those two had been dancing together all their lives." The dreamy look on Paige's face made Craig think maybe he should have paid more attention to his grandmother when she said women love to dance.

Of course, Lila Baron had also said that women love a man who plays the piano and none of his siblings ever bothered with piano lessons either. Except Mitch at one point, and Craig wasn't all that sure his brother ever made it passed "Heart and Soul."

"Oh, wow." Kyle's eyes widened. "How did I miss that those two can dance?"

Paige shrugged and stuck her open palm out. "Sucker. Might as well pay up now."

"Dance floor is still crowded." Mitch shook his head at her. The words were barely out of his mouth when one couple after another began walking away from the floor and forming a circle instead.

Sure enough, within minutes they had a clear view of Eve and Jared gliding around, their bodies moving in easy synchronization. Jared twirled her around as they circled the floor, then led her out and back into his arms. When the song ended, he lowered her into a crowd-pleasing dip and, before Craig had time to raise his hands in applause, his sister Paige gasped.

At first he thought perhaps some critter had run by and startled her, but then he realized her gaze was still fixed on the dance floor. Another second and he could see why the crowd had gone pin silent.

On one knee, Jared stared up at Eve and held an open ring box.

"Well, I'll be."

"Shh." Paige jabbed him. Though he didn't know why. From this distance all the silence in the world wouldn't make what Jared said easy to hear. By now, Eve's hands were covering her mouth, her head was nodding, and he was pretty sure a tear or two was trickling down her cheek.

Another second, and the box set aside, the ring was slid onto her finger and now the entire party was cheering in earnest.

Craig had to admit, he was thrilled for his sister. He had honestly never seen her looking as happy as she has been the last few months, and at this moment, she radiated joy. Thoughts of marriage and family truly didn't cross his mind. His work was time and travel intensive, and settling down with a wife and family simply wasn't on his agenda. Now, looking at Eve toss her arms around Jared and the two kissing as if they were the only people in the world, and more importantly, the only two that mattered, he couldn't help but think maybe it was time to rethink his agenda.

Enjoy an excerpt from
Just One Take

No one ever mentioned how young old age starts. Craig Baron took a long swallow of cool water. Rebuilding the bull-proof fence line between the Baron and Gold ranches was proving to be a bit more challenging than any of the brothers had expected.

"The old gray mare, she ain't what she used to be," Chase sang to his younger brother, a huge grin on his face. "Growing older isn't for sissies."

"Pot calling the kettle black?" Leaning on the shovel handle, Craig straightened his shoulders. "And for the record, I am neither old, nor a sissy." He wasn't even going to address the mis-assigned gender of mare.

"Speak for yourself." The eldest of today's workers, his brother Mitch pulled a traditional bandana from his back pocket and wiped his brow. "I freely admit this was way easier a decade ago."

"Ditto." Kyle, the sibling most likely to be in the best physical condition, chugged a bottle of water, then squeezing it, he tossed it into the nearby bin. "I think fence digging is for the next generation."

"And car racing?" One brow arched high on Jared Gold's—soon to be an official member of the Baron clan thanks to Craig's sister Eve—forehead.

Kyle blew out a long sigh. "It's not official yet, but," his gaze lifted to a point in the distance, "I think it's time to hang up my helmet."

Having taken another long gulp of water, Craig almost spit out his drink. His entire life, every single Baron family member had a competitive streak as wide as the Nile. Each and every one of them strived to be at the top of their game, no matter what it took to get there. The idea of Kyle walking away from racing was as absurd as Craig walking away from an award winning film. Not happening. "Are you kidding?"

"Nope." Kyle removed his hat and slapped the dust off against his thigh before placing it back on his head. "I think it's time."

"Wow." Mitch shook his head. "I know you've been hinting at it, but didn't expect to see it actually happen. At least not yet."

"Like I said," Kyle grabbed hold of one side of the two man auger for digging deeper post holes, "nothing's official yet. Might need to give Gibs another year."

"Unless someone moves over." Craig waved his fingers. "I've heard rumors that Bergeron isn't happy with his team. He's not as good as you, but he's close."

"Hmm," Kyle muttered.

From what Craig could see, his brother might think he was ready to hang up his racing suit, but maybe not so much ready to be replaced. Heaven knew Craig and Kyle weren't that far apart in years, and yet Craig was just beginning to reap the benefits of his hard work. Making it to the top of the movie industry was not any easier than climbing to the top of the racing world. He couldn't fathom Kyle walking away any more than he could fathom not fighting tooth and nail for that next big film that would make Baron Productions the holy grail of the industry. The company that A listers would be chasing after him to produce instead of the other way around. Biting his tongue, he shook his head. No way could Kyle walk away.

Jared took a minute to survey their work for the day, then glanced up at the sky. "Heat's starting to bear down on us."

"This is Texas," sarcasm dripped from Kyle's words. "The heat is always bearing down on us."

Jared chuckled. "True, but in today's case, I think we've made nice progress. This would be a good place to call it a day and pick up again tomorrow."

Craig's back twinged at the mere mention of doing this again tomorrow. He really had let his desk job make him soft. "I admit, right about now, Hazel's French cream crumb cake and a cool glass of blueberry lemonade sounds heavenly."

Staring off into the distance, Mitch's head whipped around. "Hazel made French cream crumb cake?"

The man had his moments. Just when Craig thought his older brother was totally in his own little world, he'd perk up and let everyone know he was right in step with the conversation even if he'd not said a word. The man had also been spending a great deal more of his time at the ranch than usual. Mitch would fly back and forth to DC to conduct Senate business, and then scurry home again for as long as he could. Every last member of the family considered the ranch home base and on any given weekend at least half of them would arrive and settle into their old rooms as if not a day had passed since their childhoods spending summers and weekends with the grandparents. Still, Craig wasn't sure when was the last time Mitch had made even a short pit stop at his downtown home. Almost every weekend, sometimes weekdays too, he could be found in the barns.

Despite their best efforts to subtly uncover what, if anything, was bothering Mitch, none of the brothers had been able to learn why he was spending more time than usual on the ranch the last few months. The ache beginning to poke at Craig's lower back reminded him that about now a good hot shower was in order. He could pick up worrying about his big brother another day.

"Last one back to the ranch is a rotten egg." Of course Kyle had to reduce everything to a race. The man might think he was ready to retire from the adrenaline rush of the racing world, but Craig was yet to be convinced.

In record time the entire family made it back to the ranch for that long hot shower, a change into clean clothes, and a short respite before dinner with the Governor and Grams. Even Jared and Eve joined them for the family meal.

"Any news on a date yet?" stroking the pup nestled at her side, their grandmother casually asked her granddaughter. Much the same way she'd managed to ask every week since Jared got down in front of the entire family on bended knee and proposed.

"I want to look at a few more halls before we narrow down availabilities," Eve answered just as casually as she had each and every other time her grandmother had asked the same question.

The truth was that he knew his sister was still waiting on their mother to give Eve a window when she could abandon her hideaway in Europe to brave another family wedding. Since tension tended to run high when it came to the Barons and their mother—the first ex Mrs. Bradley Baron—his sweet kid sister willingly took the flack.

"I understand Paige's plans for making the winery available as a wedding venue are coming along well. Perhaps that would be a good fit?" His grandmother's dimples deepened as the corners of her mouth lifted into a teasing smile. "I could pull a few strings if you like."

Eve's broad grin widened to match her grandmother's. "I might have a few strings of my own I could pull."

"What strings are we pulling now?" Paige, the aforementioned sister—daughter of the second ex Mrs. Bradley Baron—fluttered into the room, immediately planting a kiss on her granmother's cheek.

Smiling up at her granddaughter, Lila Baron waved her arm at Eve. "For a wedding at the vineyard."

Paige's gaze whipped around to Eve. "You interested?"

Lips pressed tightly together, the corners of Eve's mouth began to tip upward as she bobbed her head slowly. "Maybe."

Slapping her hands together with enthusiasm, Paige took her seat and leveling her gaze with her older sister, waved a finger at her. "After dinner. We'll talk."

The two siblings grinned at each other like the little girls at the table he remembered from so long ago. Though he knew there had been a lot of discussion on Paige's ambitions for the family winery, somehow, he hadn't realized she'd made enough progress to host a Baron family wedding.

"Where are you filming this week?" The Governor sliced his beef tenderloin, and stabbing at the piece, held it on the fork dangling in midair, waiting for Craig's response.

"Vancouver."

"Long flight."

Craig nodded. Didn't he know it. As Executive Producer he didn't need to be on set for filming every minute of every day, but his grandfather had taught him a long time ago that the only way to get ahead of the next guy was to work twice as hard. Besides that, the old man had also taught them all that the best way to avoid unpleasant surprises was to always keep at least one eye on any project. Whether business or pleasure, Craig had done just that, and more than once it had saved his bacon.

"Any luck with that option you were telling us about?"

Craig had to think which the heck option was his grandfather talking about.

"You know," his grandfather continued, as if he'd read Craig's mind, "that actress who lives near Austin that you were so excited about."

Oh yes. The difficult diva from Austin who no longer considered starring in movies filmed outside of her state, and who just happened to own the rights to the hottest commodity out there at the moment. The potential golden goose. A slam dunk for an Oscar nomination if handled correctly, which his production company would do, and the movie that would be the ultimate deal to put him at the top. "Still a negotiation in progress."

"Texas studio still the sticking point?" Holding a glass of water, the Governor lifted it to his lips in a show of casual chit chat when in fact, much like his grandmother's approach to Eve's wedding, there was nothing casual at all about the question.

Craig nodded. One of many where this particular diva was concerned.

"A studio closer to home wouldn't be a bad thing. Give it any more thought?"

"Some." That was most likely not the response his grandfather wanted, but it was the truth. Or at least part of the truth. With productions often running simultaneously all across the country, and his constantly catching red-eye flights to keep up, he'd more than thought about it. Including the expense and headache of undertaking the kind of project he would need, especially his preferred location in or near Houston and the ranch—a part of the country that was virtually a production desert. Austin was closer to his condo, but considering he spent more free time at the ranch than his own place, and that the cost and availability of land in the popular metroplex was beyond prohibitive, even for a Baron, that option was out of the question. Which left the idea of instead focusing on Dallas, a city that would bring him closer to his brother Chase, and that already had a healthy pool of industry professionals. Despite the head start the North Texas location offered, he couldn't bring himself to be enthused about driving four hours to visit family and the ranch any more than sitting on a plane for that amount of time. So instead, he'd done his best to charm the diva out of Texas—so far to no avail.

"You do know that the legislature has just passed approval for new tax incentives for just this type of project?"

He couldn't help but lift his gaze to meet his grandfather's. Honestly, he hadn't paid any attention to whether or not the State of Texas had perks lined up for such a project. "I'll have to look into it."

The Governor gave a single dip of his chin. "There's a folder with the highlights in my office. If you're interested, you can take a look after dinner. There also may be a few property suggestions your cousin Devlin left in the same folder."

Again, Craig nodded. Whether he was interested or not, which he was most definitely at least curious, a suggestion from the Governor might as well have been a military order. The civilian equivalent of *voluntold*. The military concept of being told to volunteer was not lost on his family. Of course, now the question that ricocheted in his mind was whether or not this particular idea would be the Holy Grail solution to his travel exhaustion and negotiation frustrations, or a suicide mission.

"Next time anyone shouts road trip after a plethora of chocolate martinis, remind me to insist we at least stay in the state of Texas." Kathleen Elizabeth Donovan, more commonly known by Kate, was most definitely a through and through extrovert with a side of gypsy. She was also getting too old to sit in a car for most of the day after joining her friends on a spontaneous trip across two states.

"Are you saying you didn't like the hot springs?" Joan, her best friend since kindergarten, didn't bother to take her attention away from the road ahead. Most likely because Joan already knew the answer.

"You know I loved every relaxing minute." And she had. Whether it was the refrigerator that insisted on freezing your milk, the neighbor's teen whose high school band chose the middle of your online meeting to practice Metallica songs, badly, or some moron who didn't understand why you couldn't play with nesting sea turtles, some days life just came at your from every direction. Not till three whole days in the peace and quiet that Mother Nature intended and all the little critters that came with it did Kate realize just how draining the real world had become. "We really do need to escape more often."

"Amen to that. Though it would help if you spent at least a fraction of the time you spend saving the world on pampering yourself."

"Maybe." She couldn't say much more, after all, Joan had a good point. For as long as Kate could remember, she worried more about helpless and abandoned animals than humans. Not everyone had the privilege of growing up and making their passion their career. She just wished having become a successful environmentalist didn't include having to deal with the money loving, profit above all, side of society. Preserving at risk species and their natural environment had proven to be a lot more demanding than fostering a few abandoned kittens when she was nine. Even so, she wouldn't change a thing—except maybe from now on a few more girls' weekends away.

Less than an hour from home, the computerized voice of the GPS stiffly instructed them to take the next exit. A quick glance at the map and the long line of orange then red along the freeway explained why. Within moments of the redirection, traffic began to slow just as they approached the suggested exit.

Joan shook her head and sighed. "I suppose the extra twenty minutes this little detour is going to cost us is less than the time we'd lose if we stayed on the freeway."

"No doubt." For the next few minutes they followed the service road and could see the parking lot the freeway had become. "I feel sorry for those folks. From the looks of it, they're going to be sitting there a good long while."

"Thank heavens for whoever invented GPS. I think I'll have a glass of wine when we get home in his—or her—honor."

"Ditto." Kate chuckled. Her head resting back against the seat, she took in the spray of pinks and reds and oranges splattered across the sky as the sun lowered itself behind the treetop canopy ahead. The little detour had taken them far from the freeway and deep into the countryside. It had been ages since she'd seen so many stars in the evening sky. Light pollution in Houston had hidden the stars for as long as she could remember.

Keeping her gaze on the treetops under the moonlight, a bird in flight caught her eye. The wingspread was impressive and the graceful movement of the bird soaring about brought a smile to her face. For Kate, watching nature's animals roam, or in this case fly, free in their natural habitat was as relaxing as the time they'd spent soaking in the natural hot springs. Her heart beat happily when what she now realized was an owl, landed on a low hanging branch down the road.

"Did you see that?" Joan waved an arm in the direction of the owl.

"I did. Magnificent."

As they grew closer, Joan's car was nearly underneath him when Kate realized which species of owl had been putting on a show for them. If she wasn't mistaken, this particular owl was one of the endangered breeds on a protective list in Texas. Mostly because to the best of her knowledge, these guys rarely ventured west of Louisiana. As if the birds had a visible map to follow, they almost always stopped at the state line.

"Ooh, there he goes." Arm extended, Joan's finger dangled in the direction the bird had flown.

Taking in a deep sigh, Kate knew she needed to follow up on the bird. Every instinct she had, and she had good ones when it came to wild life, she knew she needed to determine where this bird was calling home. Her arm straight and her finger extended, she pointed at a dirt road just beyond the tree. "Follow that bird."

Joan slowed and for the first time since turning off the freeway onto the lonely, dark, unlit country road, turned to Kate. "You've got to be kidding?"

Shaking her head vehemently, she continued to point ahead. "I have to find out of he's tagged and protected."

Joan's deep sigh filled the small car. "I guess I should be thankful you didn't find any endangered animals before we crossed the state line. I mean, I'm assuming the reason we're following that poor bird is because it's endangered?"

"Maybe."

This time deep creases filled Joan's forehead as she turned off the two lane road. "Please don't tell me you feel like bird watching for the heck of it?"

"Of course not."

"You do know that you're off duty, right?"

"No such thing." Saving the planet was not a nine to five job like a receptionist at a law firm. She cared about all the animals everywhere, even if she couldn't help them all.

"Right." Joan winced as her budget sedan bounced over the unleveled dirt. "Oh, I hope we don't need AAA. They'll never find us out here."

For a moment, Kate lost sight of the owl and then, as if

he knew she was looking for him, the bird did a near dive and flew across the front of their car.

"I'm guessing this is private property." Joan practically hugged the steering wheel as she scanned their surroundings and winced louder with each pothole they hit. "If some old geezer comes out and shoots me, you get to explain to my parents why this bird is so important."

For a brief moment the visual of an aging rancher with a corn cob pipe, overalls, and a shotgun the size of Texas almost had Kate reconsidering the folly of their pursuit. Almost. "I'm sure we'll be fine. Any self respecting rancher or farmer went to bed with the chickens."

"I sure hope they know that."

"There!" Kate pointed to cluster of buildings across an overgrown field that the owl had disappeared into. "That must be where she's nesting."

"I thought it was a he?" Joan's voice squealed as her car did another bounce.

"He, she, does it matter?"

"Only to its mate." The tease was back in her friend's banter.

Now all she had to figure out was how in the heck were they going to cross the field and find his or her nest in the pitch of night? And more importantly, without Joan killing her!

Read more of Just One Take available now

MEET CHRIS

Author of dozens of contemporary novels, including the award winning Aloha Series, Chris Keniston lives in suburban Dallas with her husband, two human children, and two canine children. Though she loves her puppies equally, she admits being especially attached to her German Shepherd rescue. After all, even dogs deserve a happily ever after.

More on Chris and her books can be found at www.chris keniston.com.

Follow Chris on facebook at ChrisKenistonAuthor or on twitter @ckenistonauthor.

Join Chris' newsletter! Enjoy inside peeks and photographs from Chris' world and stories. Some times she'll thank her subscribers with a free copy of a new 99 cent flirt.

Please, if you enjoyed reading Just One Dance, consider helping other readers find the Billionaire Barons of Texas Series by taking a moment to leave a review. Reviews are a blessing to authors and readers alike. Even just a few words will do! Thank you.

www.ingramcontent.com/pod-product-compliance
Lightning Source LLC
Chambersburg PA
CBHW031337060726
47590CB00007B/2517